The Space Between Time

The Space Between Time

Also by Bruce Macfarlane

The Space Between Time

The fourth book from
The Time Travel Diaries of
James Urquhart and Elizabeth Bicester

by

Bruce Macfarlane

2nd Edition

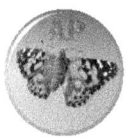

Aldwick Publishing

The Space Between Time

This is a work of fiction. Names, characters, places, and incidents are either the product of the author's imagination or are used fictitiously.

Copyright © 2018 Bruce Macfarlane
Aldwick Publishing
www.aldwickpublishing.com
All rights reserved.

ISBN-978-1-9164024-4-7

Dedication

To my wife, Julia

Preface

In these extracts from the Time Travel Diaries we find the intrepid couple enjoying a peaceful and romantic picnic by the River Rother when a motor launch turns up complete with Mr Wells.

Apparently, a certain Mr Tesla has conducted one of his electro-magnetic experiments which has fractured time and dumped everyone in an alternative world of 1895. The problem is that only a few people have noticed the difference.

Mr Wells wondered if James and Elizabeth would like to help.

The Space Between Time

Contents

Acknowledgements

Images & Illustrations.

Art work and photographs by author using digital manipulation PicsArt Photo Studio for Android and PaintShop Pro.

Book Cover:
Author's own artwork using PicsArt and PaintShop Pro

The Space Between Time

Prologue

As is well known to those of you who subscribe to my media feed, the original diaries were found together in a copper chest in the attic of a lodge at Hamgreen. They purport to be the diaries of a James Urquhart, minor science lecturer, living in 2015 and an Elizabeth Bicester, whom he claims he met at a cricket match at Hamgreen in 1873.

After spending some considerable time trying to assemble the diaries into a meaningful chronology to test their authenticity, I am now drawn to the conclusion that the diarists could not only travel in time but may have existed simultaneously in many alternative worlds.

In this volume of the diaries the couple find themselves transported back to 1895. But it is not the world they knew. An experiment with electromagnetism by a Mr Tesla has caused a shift across time to an alternative world where contact with Mars has been lost.

As usual in my narrations of the diaries I have assigned a J. for James Urquhart and E. for Elizabeth Bicester.

T W Rolleston.
Weber Institute,
Mons Olympus,
Mars.

The Space Between Time

Part 1

An Afternoon on the River

Chapter One

E.

The mist was already rising in the warm morning sun heralding a fine day and the young leaves of the dark beech woods through which we passed sparkled with their iridescent spring green.

We were travelling in James' new yellow electric carriage over the Downs towards the river by the village of Stedham where I hoped to show him a secret place of my childhood.

After my exploits of piloting the Martian spaceship James considered I had gained sufficient expertise to drive his carriage. I must say it was surprisingly easy. Only two pedals and a wheel to steer by. No wonder he found a dog cart such a challenge. I will remember to go easy on him next time he must drive one - or ride a horse.

The roads were incredibly smooth, no ruts and few potholes, and demarcated by lines to indicate which side to drive, which I was gratified to see that most of the carriages we encountered followed.

We had decided not to use the navigation system as the lady who spoke the directions causes me some annoyance. I am not quite sure how she persuades James to take guidance without question. Usually if I am performing this task while reading a map an argument on the veracity of my instructions ensues. I mentioned this to his sister once after a particularly exasperating journey along sunken roads to a holiday accommodation in Cornwall where we arrived over two hours late. She informed that the reason is simple: the lady does not answer back.

"So where and when are you taking me?" James said, nudging the steering wheel a little to assist me in avoiding a pheasant which had launched a suicidal flight out of a hedge towards us.

"You must wait. It is a surprise."

"No clues?"

"It is a special place where you will be only the second person to know of it."

As we emerged from the wood and followed a bend in the road, managing to stay mostly on the left side with only a little help and advice, the old Hall, now renovated in that mock Tudor which had become so popular in the early years of James' century, appeared behind an ash copse.

"I think it is the next road on the right." I said.

We turned down a narrow road until we had passed a green and found the old church of St. Isabel's. Unfortunately, the highway, which I wished to take, which in my time was easily traversed by a Hanson cab, had become an overgrown, sunken, green track barred by a metal gate.

He noticed my disappointment and said, "Don't worry. Luckily, it's signposted as a public bridleway. Park the car and we can walk. I'll grab the picnic out of the boot."

Parking was a little more difficult and I must admit he was quite forgiving of my difficulties in extricating his new carriage from a small ditch which I had not noticed.

We changed into our walking boots. One of the many pleasures of his world are comfortable shoes. Even those of fashion are designed to allow one to dance all night at an engagement without completely blistering and chafing one's feet. As we opened the gate and entered the old road I noticed immediately its decay and neglect. The sandstone stone walls which once lined the road and held the fields and springs at bay were now covered in green moss and broken by the roots of beech, chestnut and holly which, unattended, had grown to form a dark canopy over the track.

I could tell he was a little reticent regarding my direction but despite the changes of a hundred years I knew and felt the familiarity of the path. After about a hundred yards in which we avoided reasonably successfully three bogs, and a stream, and received only a little mud on my skirts, we arrived at an open field.

As we emerged, a soft breeze blew through the trees rustling the leaves above. For some reason, for which only later I understood, James was quite taken aback by this and grasped my hand tightly. However, on enquiry regarding his concern he dismissed it quickly although I noticed his hand did not loosen its grip. As I regarded the country before me I was gratified to find little had changed. Downs sheep still grazed the field and as I led him along a grass path to the bank of the chalk river strewn with spring flowers, yellow brimstone and chalk blue butterflies rose fluttering in the warm air and bumble bees gathered pollen from the cowslips.

And there, just as I remembered it, was the old willow, its long trailing branches, like thin fingers, caressing the flowing waters.

"You know," he said, still holding my hand, "I've walked all over the Downs and never seen so much nature gathered in one place. It's an ecologist's paradise. I'm surprised it's not on the SSSI list."

Sometimes I must gently prise him from his scientific world. I whispered in his ear. "Do you not like it, James?"

He released his hand and placing it around my waist drew me to him. "Is this your secret place?"

"Yes. And this is my favourite season."

"And you chose me to show it to." He pulled me closer and kissed me gently. He had responded as I wished.

We sat down and prepared the luncheon on the river bank. James had bought it in a wicker basket complete with willow pattern plates. They were a fashion in his time. A quest for a time lost, I presume. He had thought they remind me of my Victorian world but I had not the heart to tell him that in my time they were so common they were regularly given away to small charities for the 'Aunt Sally' at village fairs.

As we enjoyed the sandwiches and shared James' cold steak pie we suddenly heard the sound of a puffing engine and looking up saw, emerging from under a crack willow, a small steam launch.

"Good God!" said James, his eyes wide with excitement, "you know, I've never seen a boat on this river. And the first one I see is a real live steam boat! Look at the polish on that wood! And the brass and copper! I must take some photos."

He quickly retrieved his 'phone from his pocket and began to record pictures. This device is a wonder. Not only can it be used for wireless communication but also provides James with fonts of knowledge. I have come to believe it is very precious to him for it rarely leaves his person and to borrow it, even for a moment, has often took more than a little persuasion. His sister Jill, with a little ribbing, tells me that in the hands of certain ladies that James has known, its contents would be worth a fortune.

As the launch came abreast, it slowed and from the cabin a gentleman appeared who seemed to be dressed in sympathy with the age of the boat. He waved to us and in similar spirit we returned his gesture.

This caused the gentleman, for some reason, to become quite animated and gave the impression he wished to converse. We beckoned him to the bank, thinking he was in need of assistance and the launch duly turned and came to a halt beside us releasing a fair quantity of steam in the process. Then with a small leap he alighted from the launch.

My exclamation was almost as loud as James' for before us

standing in blue blazer and cap was Mr H.G. Wells.

J.

It seems we're fated not to have a peaceful life. One moment I was lying on a bank by a river with the love of my life enjoying the pleasure of her gift to me and eating an excellent pie and the next moment I'd been jolted out of time again by Wells.

"Good afternoon, Mr and Mrs Urquhart. I presume you are both married in this world. Are you well? I was hoping I would find you here."

I ignored his questions and said with quite a bit of annoyance, not least because his appearance usually resulted in some mad adventure: "What the hell are you doing here? I thought you lived in 1895."

"It is 1895, Mr Urquhart."

I suddenly realised why I hadn't come across this place before. There was no place left in my time with this amount of nature. I whispered to Elizabeth, "I suspected when I felt that breeze again that something strange was going to happen."

"What did you mean? Have you felt it before?"

"Yes, just before I first met you at Hamgreen."

"You mean? Oh! No wonder you held my hand so tightly."

I turned back to Wells. "How did you know we'd be here?"

"You are watched all the time."

He caught the meaning of my look.

"I do not mean as a voyeur but your paths through time and space are known to our little friends."

"Ah, the Martians." I said, and a fleeting vision of one of those small white ghostly rabbit-like creatures came to mind. They are almost ethereal in appearance for unlike us they exist a little in the past and future with the aid of their gossamer wings.

"So, what are they after now?" I said, not looking forward to the reply, "We know, once they and you get together it seems - how can I put this politely -, '*opportunities*' come to Elizabeth and me."

"I confess I do have an opportunity for you. But first you must join me."

"What! on that boat?"

I felt Elizabeth's hand reach and grasp mine. Wells noticed and said, "We will not be going far."

"You're right," I said, "We're staying right here."

"I assure you it is but a small journey." He was obviously trying to engage my curiosity and to my annoyance I found he had partially succeeded.

"This journey, is it in time or space?"

"James!" hissed Elizabeth, her eyes wide and tightening her grip on my hand, "What are you saying?"

"Sorry. Shall we go back to the road and home?"

"Yes! For I feel our success in these adventures depends too much on Lady Luck and in my experience of her she is very fickle."

As we stood up to pack our lunch and refuse Wells' offer he raised his hand and said, "I must apologise but I am afraid the boundary betwixt here and your home has temporarily vanished."

I wondered what he meant by 'temporary'. There was a lot of 'time' in that word. But before I could ask how much, Elizabeth said to Wells, "If I understand you correctly, are you saying that if we retraced our steps back to the highway we would find ourselves still in this time?"

"That is correct, Mrs Urquhart."

"So, you mean we have no choice but to follow you?" I

said.

"I am afraid that is the case."

Elizabeth was visibly upset to the point of almost crying and shouted, "You have ruined my day! You know James and I... I mean we are of different times. Every moment is precious to us."

She looked at me for support which I gave by drawing my arm around her.

She continued, her voice now shaking, "At any moment, through things we do not understand, we could be sent back to our own times, never to know each other again! Why do you not leave us alone?"

I couldn't have put it better. Though to hear it from the one I loved melted my heart. Nevertheless I knew we had no option but to follow him if we were to get out of this time. I said to Wells, with my arm still tightly around her, "So where are we really going?"

"Why, to Midhurst."

"In that boat?"

"In this time, Mr Urquhart, it is quicker and easier than the roads."

But Elizabeth was not to be persuaded.

"James! I am not going! We will go back to Stedham, hail a cab and go to my home to find a way back."

"We can't! Look at our clothes. I like your dress but I don't think the good people of Stedham are going to, especially on a Sunday. You'll be arrested as soon as we arrive."

She stared down at her dress which only just covered her knees.

"Oh, you men. You only think of one thing."

"No, that's not quite true." I said, savouring that enjoyable thought when I suddenly remembered a book of Wells and that the village of Iping was just down the road.

"There is another reason for not going back," I said, "We don't want to meet the Invisible Man, do we, Wells?"

"What do you mean?" she said.

"Our dear friend here," I said, pointing at Wells, "wrote a book about such a man who came from Iping just down the road."

"And why should that be a worry?"

"Because as you know, the things he writes about are often based on real events. Isn't that right, Wells?"

Wells shrugged his shoulders and said nothing.

"But if he is real," she said, scanning the countryside, "how can he be seen?"

"When he wanted to be seen he wrapped himself in bandages like a mummy."

"Is this true, Mr Wells?" she said.

"A different world, Mrs Urquhart. Are you coming? There is not much time."

Elizabeth looked back at the woods we had come from, "I still want to go home whether there is an invisible man or not!"

"Look," I said, whispering in her ear. "If we go to Midhurst, we may be able to get to the time cavern and escape from there."

She hesitated then with a sigh said, "You are right. If we cannot go back. We will take our chances in Midhurst."

And so we gathered up our picnic and the remainder of my pie and followed Wells on to the boat.

12

Chapter Two

E.

The time cavern under the ruined Norman castle at Midhurst is a mystery which has affected much of our lives together. We had found it accidentally after exploring the passage from the White Room at the Spread Eagle Coaching Inn. It is difficult to describe for it changes shape. I believe it is a roughly hewn cave about fifty feet in diameter within which are machines for controlling time and space and often contains two large globes, one of Earth and the other of Mars. By means of pointers on the spheres the cavern, we can move across the two planets. Sometimes doors appear in the walls of the cavern which allow access to different places or time on the two planets.

We do not know who built it or why but on many adventures it has served as a portal to when or where we wished or did not wished to go. We believe it was built by the Martians as part of their transport system between our two planets. Mr Wells, I am sure has much knowledge of it.

However, we were trapped in 1895 and James suggestion that we should take our chance with it to return home seemed the only possible escape.

After I had boarded the launch and managed to pull James on board and into the cockpit, I discovered he had a similar affinity with small boats as with horses and an alarming tendency to fall off both.

Mr Wells said, "Before we start, you might wish to change your clothes. I have provided what I hope is suitable attire in the cabin."

He opened the door where we saw on the table two piles of

14

carefully folded clothing of the late nineteenth century including undergarments, which on inspection, suggested mine had been designed for a bordello rather than for boating on the river. James noticed as well "Hmh! Nice choice of underwear. Look forward to seeing you in them."

As I had no intention of exchanging my soft and comfortable twentieth century undergarments for those of the nineteenth, he was a little disappointed by my reply.

However, Wells, on hearing my response, was a little crestfallen and apologised for their unsuitability saying he was assured by my sister they were my favourite things.

The mention of my sister explained the garments before me. Flory was never one to miss an opportunity for a joke at my expense. However, her welfare was of more concern. Wells replied to my inquiry about this with: "She is in good health and still lives in Hamgreen. We may have time to visit but for now we must hurry for there is much to do."

The other clothes Flory had provided were acceptable. A white blouse with thankfully small mutton chop sleeves and a straight, lightly pleated, dark green skirt. I was pleased to find bustles were out of fashion. The jacket was short and practical. As for the hat - well, it sufficed. Poor James, however, was provided with beige corduroy breeches and a grey sack coat. I will not repeat the comments he made regarding my sister's virtue nor on the remains of mine when I said he would look very fetching in the mustard stockings.

When we had dressed, we returned to the cockpit where Mr. Wells was regarding the river bank.

On hearing us, he turned and reaching into a pocket within his jacket produced a brown leather wallet.

"I presume on your excursion, not expecting this adventure, you omitted to bring monies of this period. So, I have provided a sum of £50 for your expenses."

He then handed it to James, who immediately opened the wallet and after counting the contents provided me with half.

"You take this, Elizabeth, just in case we get separated or I lose the wallet. And," humorously wagging a finger at me, "don't spend it all on clothes this time."

"I can assure you that if I am in need of replacement on occasion of another of your adventures," She said, carefully putting the monies in my pocketbook, "it will be your half which I will use for assistance."

Mr Wells made no comment although I could see he was a little confused by this banter. He then withdrew his fob watch from another pocket and with a cursory glance at it and then to our dress said, "We must hurry. If you are ready, we will begin." And without waiting for a reply he opened a valve which caused a gush of steam to explode from the funnel, nearly frightening us out of our wits, and the launch began to chug slowly downstream.

J.

It was a long time since I'd been on a small boat. The last time was in a Laser off the coast of Hartlepool, where it sank. It has a wooden dam board at the back which you lift to let the sea out and close to keep it out. Apparently if you do this the wrong way around the boat fills with sea water and sinks. So, I wasn't too keen to get on another one. Not least because I hadn't considered Wells as a seafarer. Once I'd got into the cockpit, encouraged by some unsympathetic banter by my nearest and dearest, followed by more when I got into her father's ill-fitting clothes, we started moving. There followed a lot of wobbling to and fro which, for some reason, was reduced considerably when Elizabeth sat me down on the bench and told me to stay there.

As we moved down the river, I began to appreciate how much wildlife had been lost in the space of only a hundred years. I saw more kingfishers and water voles than I'd seen in the whole of my life, and here and there between the crack willows, lush grass water meadows appeared with their small zigzagging streams twinkling in the sunlight. Then as we approached Easebourne, couples in rowing boats began to appear in their Victorian Sunday best. It was an idyllic scene straight out of an impressionist painting. Elizabeth sat down beside me and for a few minutes we sat enjoying this dreamlike scene almost forgetting we were on one of Wells' quests. However, it was not to last for as we wove through the boats, waving and smiling, I began to hear behind us quite a lot of raised voices. Looking back, I saw the reason. The bow waves produced by Wells' boat had turned the peaceful river into a sea of bobbing boats and flaying oars and in the process, judging by the sound of arguments between the couples in the boats, had possibly ended the romantic intentions of quite a few. For the next twenty minutes Elizabeth and I kept our heads down and pretended we were deep in conversation and impervious to the mayhem around us.

By the time we reached the ruins of Cowdray it seemed like the whole of Midhurst had taken to boating on the river and were determined to impede our every movement. Wells, however, was not to be deterred and steadfastly ploughed through them like an ice-breaker. Elizabeth said she'd never heard such language on a Sunday. However, when I asked her jokingly what days of the week she normally heard such language she said, only when I had work to do on our cottage. A bit unfair, I thought. Eventually Wells broke through the throng and brought the boat to a quiet jetty by the ruins of the old Norman castle.

When I had got off the boat on to dry land with Elizabeth's

help I said, "So Wells, what have you in store for us? A Time machine or a trip to the time cavern?"

"It is Sunday, Mr Urquhart. We are going to church."

E.

With my ears still burning from the language I helped James on to the jetty, then noticing his appearance, re-buttoned his shirt so they matched the holes, adjusted the wings of his collar, re-tied his cravat and told him to pull up his left stocking. Eventually I was satisfied that if we met any acquaintances, I would be able to pass him off as my husband without too much comment. I do sometimes wonder how men are ever able to dress themselves without assistance. I remember discussing this with Jill one afternoon while James was asleep on the sofa in his gardening attire, or as he called them, his 'comfortable' clothes. She thought that although her snoring brother might be an exception most men are perfectly capable of dressing themselves but some purposely use this as a ruse to attract a sympathetic and dutiful lady. Noticing my look, she said that I should not think James was capable of such a thing as that would require effort on his part. Our laughter awoke him and not a little effort was required to convince him our mirth was not at his expense. Poor James. I should record, however, that James suggested that having adjusted most of his clothing I should check he had buttoned his breeches correctly. I declined his request as I felt we had attracted enough attention for one day. Apparently, he told me, buttoned trousers had come back into fashion for a short period in his time. Not to be left out, he duly bought a pair but quickly consigned them to charity after an urgent call of nature during an exceedingly long evening at an hostelry caused him to understand why the zip fastener had become so popular.

I must apologise to any ladies who may discover and read my dairies and wonder on the variety of subjects I mention, but if you have any thoughts of marriage you may find within these pages considerable assistance in the understanding of our men folk.

But to Mr Wells and his 'opportunity' for us. Apparently, we had an appointment in St. Denys and we were not to be late. As we walked through the ruins of the castle I was gratified that that accursed time machine did not reappear, for I did not wish to play hide and seek in the brambles again and dispatch another good dress and stockings to the rag and bone man.

When we arrived at the lych-gate, Mr Wells stopped and glanced up at the church clock. "Ah! We have a little time yet. We will wait here."

The clock showed five minutes before two o'clock.

I noticed there was something different about the church upon which I could not lay my finger, but before I could remark on it, a door opened, and several parishioners came out. We made way for them, apologising for being an obstruction to their passage but for some reason they politely, or should I say rudely, ignored our presence except for one lady who seemed to be a little captivated by my male acquaintances. She wore a dark green, heavy dress gathered in by a thick belt at the waist and a white embroidered collar. Her brown hair was tightly curled beneath a small hat. He paused to acknowledge her presence in his usual fashion. "Hi, do we know you?"

But she said nothing, possibly taken aback by his familiarity or his left stocking which was working its way down his leg again to meet his ankle. Instead she put her hand out to touch him. For some reason, I instinctively put my arm through his and pulled him away a little but the lady did not seem to notice and continued to try and reach out to him! He was now looking distinctly worried but as he turned to me for help she withdrew her hand and looking a little perplexed, turned and joined the other parishioners.

"God, Elizabeth! What happened there?"

"I do not know. You do not look completely out of place apart from your stocking. Though perhaps your clean shaven and hatless visage coupled with your unoiled hair may have fascinated her."

"And I'd presumed it was my handsome looks and magnetic personality," he said, pretending to be crestfallen. I responded in kind.

"On the first, as your dutiful wife, I could not possibly disagree but on the second I confess I am a little influenced by your sister and still withhold judgement."

His response reminded me of what protection the bustle afforded to a lady's rear but also drew my attention to Mr. Wells whom I noticed was following the woman with a puzzled expression on his face. As he gazed after her I heard him say almost under his breath, "I feel I know that woman, but..."

For the first time since I had known Mr. Wells he did not seem to be in control. He continued in the same fashion.

"I know her, I am sure," he said, still looking at her, "But I fear she is not quite of this time."

"What do you mean?" I enquired.

He turned to us, awakening from his contemplation, "For a moment I thought it was my cousin, Isabel. But she did not recognise me."

"But I felt as though I was invisible!" said James.

"Not invisible. But perhaps a little transparent, influenced by the time slip."

"Time slip! What time slip?" we said in unison and as if in reply the church clock struck two. We all turned towards it.

"Ah, I see by the clock it is time." said Mr Wells, "We must hurry!"

Mr Wells hurried us towards the church and turned the latch on the wooden studded door then disappeared into the church. With one last look at each and other and holding hands tightly, we followed.

Chapter Three

J.

We walked through the door and, unsurprisingly, found ourselves standing in the nave. Surprisingly, the familiar grey stonework had become a bright sandy colour and the gothic doors and stained-glass windows now had rounded arches. However, what really struck me was the ceiling of the nave which was now a barrel vault painted a deep blue with myriad silver and golden stars. Elizabeth said, "This is Romanesque! The old and new gothic has disappeared! Look at the pillars. Have we moved back in time?"

"I don't know. Could be. The pillars are massive and the coloured stone with all those patterned whorls reminds me of Durham Cathedral. But look at those people by the pulpit. They're dressed in the same fashions as those people outside. However," I looked around the nave, "what's worrying me is that damned enigma Wells has vanished, leaving us on our own again!"

We starred at each other, wide eyed. No words were required. We both had the same idea. But when we turned around and tried to open the door to escape, we found it wouldn't open.

Elizabeth wailed, "What puzzle is this? Why are we here? These people suggest we are still in the same time. But I am sure we did not pass through a portal!"

"I don't know." I said, feeling around the door in the hope of finding some mechanism to open it. "This is weird. And where's Wells?"

We stood for a moment scanning the nave for some clue as to what was going on but found none and tried the locked door again. Eventually Elizabeth said, "I am at a loss. There is nothing to be gained by staying here. Let us speak with those people there with the vicar and hope none of them were on those boats."

We walked over to them. The vicar was wearing the obligatory large white sideburns and beard of the learned ancient Victorian and talking about a prayer class. I politely waited until he'd finished then said to him, "Excuse me for interrupting but have you seen a gentleman in a blue coat?"

No one took any notice, and the vicar continued with his conversation. I turned to Elizabeth, presuming my twenty-first century grammar or manners were not worthy of a reply. She took her cue and said in her best sweet-demure voice, which normally gets me to do whatever she wants, "We apologise for interrupting your conversation but we have lost an acquaintance and we believe he passed through here."

They continued to ignore us. "Right!" I said, losing it a bit and talking directly to the vicar with a voice that just about echoed off the nave walls. "Would you mind talking to us because we need to find this bloke. He was wearing a blue blazer and cap. Have you seen him?"

It was at that point that Elizabeth tried to get the vicar's attention by tugging his white shawl. Her scream reverberated off the walls for her hand went straight through him as if he weren't there!

"What the..", I stopped myself just in time, remembering where I was. I tried to touch one of the parishioners and like Elizabeth my hand went through her. They continued to ignore us.

"What fantasy is this?" Elizabeth whispered, holding my arm and looking gratified that it at least was solid.

My mind was racing. I took her by the arm and slowly walked away backwards not taking my eyes off them until I felt a pillar behind me.

"What shall we do?" she said, still whispering, "They do not see or hear us! Are we invisible?"

"I don't know. And that damned door we came through is locked."

"Then we must find Mr Wells. Perhaps he has gone outside through the west door."

Seeing nothing better to do I agreed and we walked slowly and quietly towards it, for some inexplicable reason being worried that we might disturb the people who couldn't see or hear us. But as we approached the door it opened and the woman whom we'd met by the lych-gate appeared. She immediately saw us.

"Oh! You are real! Thank God!" And crossed herself. "Please help me. I arrived by tram for the morning service with my husband, but he has gone!"

"What do you mean gone?" I said, wondering what this had to do with me.

She grabbed my arm. Her face was white.

"He is nowhere to be found!"

I thought she was going to faint. It wasn't unusual for these poor Victorian women, trussed up in their corsets, restricting the oxygen and blood flow, to pass out. I presume they were designed to lend truth to the idea that women were the weaker sex.

Elizabeth also suspected she was about to pass out and came to her assistance by gently and firmly holding her arm. "What's your husband look like?"

"He was wearing a light blue blazer and cap."

I hoped for a moment that blue blazers and matching caps were all the rage in Midhurst.

"What's your name?" I asked, hoping the answer wasn't what I was expecting.

"Isabel Wells."

 This was madness. It was Wells' cousin. I asked the only question left.

"And is your husband Herbert Wells?"

"Why, yes! How do you know?"

"I know a lot about Wells. And now possibly more than he does."

"What do you mean?" she said grabbing my arm. "Who are you?"

I hesitated for a moment, wondering how much to say then said, "We are Mr and Mrs Urquhart. We are visiting Midhurst for a day on the river. We met your husband a short while ago who said he was looking for you."

Elizabeth looked at me as though I was mad. I shrugged my shoulders indicating I agreed with her. However, thankfully, this story seemed to mollify Mrs Wells for a moment.

E.

I was surprised Mr Wells was married. He never struck me that he had the slightest interest in my sex.

I asked her, trying to hide my thoughts, "When did you last see him?"

"Not more than half an hour ago. We had come for bible class. I had stopped to buy some flowers, and he went ahead into the church but when I entered, he was nowhere to be seen!"

Her obvious fragility at her loss told me that this was not the time to admit we had been with Mr. Wells for the last couple of hours. "Are you sure he came in here?" I said.

"Yes, I am sure!" she exclaimed. Her eyes darted around the nave and then pointing to our locked door, said, "I wondered if he had left by the south door for some reason and I went to explore. It was then that I thought I saw you both with my husband."

"What do you mean - you thought you saw us?" said James, a little too strongly for she flinched at his enquiry.

"You were by the lych-gate. But as I approached you," she grasped James' arm for reassurance and said," you lacked substance!"

"In what way?" pressed James.

"I cannot explain it! You were like glittering shadows which faded in and out! I suspected I was affected by his absence so chose to ignore you. I was so pleased that after searching the graveyard with no success I returned here via the west door and saw you again."

She was now quite agitated, and she had my sympathy for I am sure that in the space of a few moments if I had lost my husband and been confronted by ghostly phantoms I would be of a similar condition. I gently touched James' arm to try to desist him from further interrogation. He let out a sigh and said to her, quite kindly, "Come and sit down in a pew for a moment. We'll try and help but first I must talk to my wife in private."

We both stared at him questioningly. He saw our expressions and said to her, "Don't worry, we will be close by, just over there by the pillar, but I do need to discuss something first with my wife."

She agreed to sit down and once reassured that she was comfortable and could still see us, James took me over to one of the nave pillars and whispered, "Before we go further, first, I need to tell you about what I know about his women in my world."

"His women?" I said, somewhat taken aback, "I had not thought the fairer sex was of interest to him."

"Ha! Quite the opposite. From what I can remember of a biography I read of Wells, he was first married to his cousin

Isabel Wells – they met at her mother's house, I think – and that's who I think this woman is. Unfortunately, they didn't get on, mainly because she felt outclassed by him. Bit like me sometimes."

I was about to protest but with a smile he pressed his finger to my lips and continued, "I think it was actually this year, 1895, that he left her and shacked up with a Catherine Robbins whom I believe he eventually married."

"Who is this Catherine?"

"She was supposed to be quite a liberal person and allowed him to have a number of other women."

"I'm afraid you may not find me so receptive to such a proposition."

"Really! I'd better cancel my engagements for the weekend. However, what worries me is this. Is the Wells we met on the boat the same one she's looking for?"

"You mean the Mr Wells who brought us here may not know of these women?"

"Possibly. Or worse case. He's already legged it with Catherine, leaving us to sort out Isabel."

"I will be very disappointed if Mr Wells has dragged us away from our world just to help him with his extra-marital affairs."

"I'll add 'disappointed' to the small list of words I was thinking of."

"In that case I hope our Maker is not reading your thoughts. But what of your second point?"

"Second point? Oh, yes. I need to buy some proper trousers."

"Why?"

"These knickerbockers."

"They are breeches. But what of them? You look very fetching; if you pull up that left stocking."

"I look like an overgrown schoolboy."

"And what of me when I first came to your time, having to wear your sister's skirts that showed my all? I still remember the embarrassment of having to walk down your stairs with you waiting at the bottom."

"You weren't showing your all."

"But how would you know?" I replied, with some amusement, "You claimed you were not looking."

"Oh. Erm... Couldn't help it." He said, pretending to be crestfallen at my accusation then wagged his finger at me, "Well. It wasn't my fault. You shouldn't have such lovely legs."

"You are incorrigible. But to return to your clothes before you are further compromised. It is Sunday, James. A day of rest from Mammon. The shops are all closed."

"Then I'll have to get back to the boat."

"How? The door is locked. Besides, the cut of your clothes is of trivial importance compared to the plight of that poor woman."

After a little more persuasion, he acquiesced.

"OK, you're right. Let's go and find out what she knows about Wells. But don't mention his other women. And tomorrow I want to buy some proper trousers."

We returned to Mrs Wells who was watching us pensively. It was at that moment I noticed a gentleman dressed in a blue jacket and matching coloured cap appear from the vestry.

Chapter Four

J.

He strolled towards us as though he did not have a care in the world. I waited to find out which Wells he thought he was. I soon found out when his 'wife' on seeing him, immediately ran to him and hugged him. "Oh, Herbert! I thought I'd lost you."

Unfortunately, 'Herbert' was having difficulty responding in kind.

He gently and firmly released her and looking at her intently said, "Isabel. Is it really you?"

She looked at us then him, "Of course it is! Why do you not think it is me?"

Then he noticed us and ignoring her question said, "Hello, Mr and Mrs Urquhart. I was looking for you. Where did you go?"

I said rather sarcastically, "We've been standing in this church wondering where you'd gone and looking after your wife."

"I do not have a wife, Mr Urquhart." said Wells, looking at Mrs. Wells in complete surprise.

"This woman says she's your wife. Her name's Isabel Wells. Ring any bells?"

He took a sharp intake of breath. "It is you, Isabel! Why do you think we are married?"

Mrs Wells, having lost one husband and gained another who claimed he wasn't married to her, was beginning to feel faint again. She grabbed Wells' arms tightly, "Herbert! What is the matter? Is this some parlour trick? If it is, it is not amusing!"

He continued to gaze at her, trying to understand. "Isabel. I have not seen you in a long time. Where have you been?"

She turned to us. Fear and confusion now crossed her face, "What is happening? He does not recognise me! You must help him! Why does Herbert think we are not married!"

Wells needed to be brought up to speed. For once it seemed he really didn't know what was going on.

I grabbed his sleeve. "Wells! Listen to me! I think two time paths have overlapped. You understand what I mean."

He took a double take. "You mean there are two of me here?"

At that point Isabel fainted and fell almost backwards straight into my arms. I should note for when Elizabeth reads this that the only reason, I grabbed her by her breasts was to prevent her slipping to the floor.

We managed to get her to a pew and Elizabeth loosened her jacket and blouse. After a few seconds she came around and Wells, pausing only for a moment, reached out and held both her hands, saying, "I am sorry, Isabel. I must have succumbed to a brain fever. Please forgive me. I cannot remember anything. Where am I?"

I must hand it to him. He catches on quickly.

E.

I tried to put things together. We came by boat with Mr Wells. We met his wife outside the church, but she could only see us faintly as though we were out of her time. Yet when we met her again in the church after passing through the door, she could see us clearly! Then, it seems, at almost the same moment we arrived with Mr Wells, Mrs Wells' husband disappeared. But then I remembered there had been a delay. We did not enter the church immediately because Mr Wells required that we wait until two of the clock before entering. Did he know what was going to happen? And what became of her husband? This needed explanation.

But to return to the problem in hand. We now had to manage Mr Wells' recently acquired brain fever for I was not convinced Mrs Wells was ready to accept that there were two of him loose in Midhurst let alone be introduced to time travel.

However, I was relieved to see she that the explanation for his disappearance had relaxed her a little although she was still on her guard, for she said to him, "Oh, Herbert. I am sorry that you are unwell, but in truth it is a relief that that there is a reason for your behaviour. But do you remember nothing? Pray tell me, can you remember what we did this morning?"

He looked at us for help. I looked at James for assistance who in turn gave me a look which suggested I had put him on the spot. However, he rose to the challenge.

James said, "Listen! Before we go any further, we need to get him home where we can treat him AND I'd like to get away from this place before we all disappear again."

"Thank you, Mr Urquhart," said Mr Wells, recovering a little more and to keep his wife's focus diverted, turned to her and said, "Will you take me home, Isabel? I do not trust myself to make a sane decision."

"Of course, I will take you home, but I would like your acquaintances to come with us."

We glanced at each other, then instinctively towards the door by which we had arrived. James went over to it, tried the handle again and returned.

"Looks like we're going with them, Elizabeth."

My heart sank. Each turn seemed to be taking us deeper into a labyrinth.

We all left the church by the west door and walked into bright sunlight across a walled, flagstoned quadrangle and passed through an arch into the main street. To my surprise, it was lined with soot-covered buildings and houses of a Mediterranean style with red pantile roofs. As we stepped on to the cobbled road, I immediately smelt a familiar aroma in the air and realised it was coal smoke; so unfamiliar in James' world I had almost forgotten its pungent odour. But what held my attention was the billowing dark clouds rising to the north which reminded me of the great industrial cities around Birmingham I had passed on a train en route to Scotland.

"What can that be?" I said to James, pointing to the horizon. Mr Wells replied, "Iron furnaces."

"In Sussex?" said James surprised, "I thought industry was banned in Sussex."

"This is a different world. The whole of the north of the county is a wasteland devoted to the retrieval of iron ore and smelting."

"But what are they using for fuel? Wood? There's no coal in Sussex." replied James.

"It comes from the coal mines of Kent."

"How?" said James.

One of his endearing and sometimes frustrating qualities is his need to know how and why things work. I confess I am of a similar persuasion. He tells me that each day between arising and returning to bed if he had not learnt something new it was not worth getting up and I could not but agree for is not each day given to us for a reason?

Mr Wells, who had not been idle in between his quests for us, said, "They have built grand canals across the county to transport the coal to the furnaces and use them to send the iron and steel to London."

"So what about the iron and steel industries in Wales and the North?"

"I am unsure. All news I have read seems to only relate to the south of England. It is though they do not exist or are of no consequence."

"Not much difference from my world then," said James, rather sarcastically, "Most southerners think civilization ends at the Watford Gap."

I had heard this phrase before in James' world. Apparently, it is generally assumed by those that live in London and its surrounds that the North of Britain begins at a place near Northampton. I am rarely admonished by James for my views for he is very tolerant on what my upbringing regarded as natural and has provided much enlightenment on the advantages of equality within our species, but when I suggested this was reasonable, he was more than a little put out. I presume by his name that one of his ancestors did come from the North and he had need to defend them.

But to return to our excursion. As we walked on to the road, we passed families and acquaintances gathered in small groups in their Sunday best but I was surprised to see they were not in black but in all the colours of the rainbow. James was so struck by their colours that he removed his phone and photographed some of them. Their clothes suggested that the period of mourning for Queen Victoria's husband had expired or perhaps she did not exist in this world. Down the centre of the cobbled road were metal rails on which, to my surprise, I saw an electric tram coming from the east. There was not a horse in sight!

I asked James if this was expected for this year for I was sure, from my reading of his histories that horse drawn trams were not replaced until the twentieth century. He agreed with my view and suggested that once again we had slipped across time. Eventually, one of the trams stopped by the church and we all followed Mrs Wells on to it. Thankfully. though inexplicably, the conductor and passengers acknowledged our presence. They also did not ask for the fare. As I sat down next to James with the Wells together behind us I whispered to James, "There is something within that church which causes a change, for out here although it is different, people are substantial."

"I agree," he responded in kind, "And I hope our own Wells knows all about it. But after seeing his surprise at seeing his wife here I'm not convinced."

"Yes. He does not seem himself," I said, "And we have still not ascertained why he has brought us here."

"I know! When we've sorted out Mrs Wells, we'll give him the third degree."

I turned around and saw Mr Wells staring out of the window lost in thought with Mrs Wells' head resting on his shoulder. She saw me and smiled as she snuggled up closer to him. I could see 'sorting out' Mrs Wells, as James put it, and her matrimonial relationship was going to require some considerable effort. Although I really could not understand what any of this had to do with us.

J.

Her home was on the edge of the village on the road to Cocking in a row of new but pleasant single-bay, white walled villas complete with small front gardens full of bluebells and hemmed in by iron railings.

Around the porch of the green painted door of her house red camellias flowered. Mrs Wells removed a key from her pocketbook which she inserted into the door and opened it. Then she turned to us and said with an almost inviting smile, "Do come into our abode. It is small but it is sufficient for our needs. Isn't it Herbert."

Herbert continued to play his amnesia card and nodded.

Once we were in the narrow hall lined with lithographs of

rustic churches and rugged landscapes, she closed the door, an turning to Wells said, "Now do you remember where you are, Herbert?"

He looked around with a puzzled expression and said, "No, I do not, Isabel."

I said quickly. "Let's get him sat down and see what we can do."

She took us into the parlour. It was decked out in heavy Victorian green and red chintz with two comfy, green upholstered chairs and a sofa all embroidered with coloured tropical birds. But what caught my attention were the electric lights. When we had sat down, I said. "Ok. First question. When are we?"

She looked puzzled by that. She turned to Wells but seeing no help there turned back to me and said, "Why, whatever do you mean? It is 1895 of course.

"I meant the exact date?

"Oh," she relaxed a little, "It is the 24th March 1895. Have you been away?"

"No more than usual. It is those things that are confusing me," I said, pointing at the electric lights.

"Oh, I see," she said. Again, she looked at Wells for assistance and got none. Then she said, rather cautiously "Why are you surprised to see electric lights here? Do you not have them?"

"Yes, we do but where or when we live…"

Elizabeth pinched my arm and just managed to stop me blurting out when we came from. Unfortunately, Mrs Wells noticed and said, "What of the lights. Why do you think…"

Luckily Elizabeth managed to change the subject. "Please forgive us but we have not properly introduced ourselves."

"Of course, I am sorry. This is my Husband Herbert, and I am his wife Isabel and we have been married for just four years."

She then gave Wells a look that suggested she'd been married to the wrong man for forty.

"And we are James and Elizabeth Urquhart, and we live in Chichester and have been married for just under a year," replied Elizabeth, who re-assuringly gently clasped my hand in a manner which suggested she was married to the right man.

"Thank you," said Mrs Wells, then, judging quite rightly I was the weaker of us two, looked me straight in the eye said, "And is it different in Chichester as well?"

"Yes. It is." I said trying to be as neutral as possible without giving anything away. For I wanted to hear here story first. However, she understood what I implied. And giving me rather a suspicious look said, "With regard to the electric lighting, as far as I understand, there were no 'Dark Ages' here. Is it the same with you?"

She'd now cornered me. However, Elizabeth interjected and said, very softly, "But surely Mrs Wells, if there were no Dark Ages how did you know that they did not exist?"

She's a bit bright, my wife. I assume a childhood absent of telly and social media must have helped and of course her use of negatives which always confuse me. Well, that's my excuse.

She'd caught Mrs Wells nicely. "You are very astute, Mrs Urquhart."

She hesitated and bit her lip then continued, "I do not know how to say this for I have already been accused of madness by my husband. But before I arrived here, I lived in a world where they did exist."

"When was that?" I said, jumping in and trying to convey the impression it was the most natural thing to ask.

"About two weeks ago. I can't quite remember. But it was March."

"What happened?"

"The world just changed. But to my consternation I seemed to be the only one who noticed."

"Not even your husband?"

"No. It was horrible." She stared at Wells pointedly who was studiously gazing around the room and pretending he wasn't listening. She continued, "I spoke to Herbert of it and he thought I had had a fit that had affected my mind. He would have none of it and when I refused to desist, he took me to a doctor who attributed it to the fragility of a woman's mind and prescribed complete rest for a week."

I turned to Elizabeth, "There you are. All you girls need if you're getting a bit fraught and emotional is good lie down for a week."

"Thank you. I will look forward to a week's holiday from cooking and housework on our return."

I quickly went back to the subject.

"And you've been unable to get back to your world?"

"That is correct. And now my husband in this world does not know me. I am alone!"

Time for Wells to answer some questions.

"What the hell is going on, Wells?"

But before he could reply, Mrs Wells interjected, "I would prefer it if you would control your language, Mr Urquhart, if not for your wife's sake then for mine."

"I would prefer it if Wells here had left me and my wife on the bank of the river this morning."

"What river, Mr Urquhart? We have not left Midhurst today."

I had now dug a deep hole. But with what seemed like no escape I decided to keep digging.

"The River Rother where Wells here," pointing at him with my finger, "picked us up on a steam boat with one of his promises of an exciting adventure."

Elizabeth was now looking at me with that 'where are you going with this' face. I reassured her by shrugging my shoulders and giving an expression of an idiot who doesn't know what he is doing.

Luckily, having come to that conclusion already, she came to my rescue, though not without first rolling her eyes up to the ceiling. "Mrs Wells, please forgive my husband, he is a little fraught and fragile and possibly needs to lie down for a week," jabbing me in the ribs with her finger. "However, you have said enough regarding your experience to allow me to recount ours of today without, I hope, causing further trepidation. Although the conclusion, I must warn you, may be difficult to comprehend."

She then carefully and succinctly went through the day's adventures. However, despite her efforts, Mrs Wells was not to be persuaded.

"I do not believe you. He was with me all morning. Have you been with that woman again?" She glared at Wells. accusingly, who from his look hadn't a clue what was going on, or was giving a very good impression of it.

"Do you mean Catherine Robbins?" I asked, throwing in a small grenade and receiving another jab from Elizabeth

"That vixen! You are well informed, Mr Urquhart."

"Not as well as I'd like to be."

Then Elizabeth said to me. "How do we know this is the Mr Wells that came with us this morning?"

"What do you mean?"

"Remember when we entered the church he vanished. Was it the same Wells who reappeared"?

"God, you're right!"

I turned to Wells. and asked him what he was doing before he came into the church.

"Why, I was with you, Mr Urquhart, on the launch."

That was reassuring although as I expected, not for Mrs Wells.

"That is a lie!" She exclaimed. "You were with me from waking until church. So how........" She caught her breath, "Wait. I think I see. Are you from my other world? Which Herbert are you?"

"I am from another world, but I am afraid it was not yours."

"Then were you not my husband in this other world?"

"No. But I wanted to be. Why did you run away?"

"I didn't. I came to visit you. And you asked to marry me. We were married!"

"No. We were not. You ran away to Wiltshire and ignored my letters."

E.

While they argued, I whispered to James, "We've been to a world like this before."

"Yes! Wasn't it the one where the clothes were made from linen and we travelled by tram?"

"And since then," I replied, "I have remembered to bring spare undergarments which are comfortable."

"And very nice they are too."

"Shh! They will hear you."

"OK. We need to distract them."

Both the Wells were still in argument and had become exceedingly vexed. Mrs Wells had the visage of a lady who had despaired of convincing her husband of her point of view and Mr Wells was a little red in the face from his exertions of denying her accusations of his extra-marital affairs.

James ignored their predicament and said to Mr Wells, "So now we know which Wells you are, you can tell us why you brought us here? It obviously wasn't to find your wife, otherwise you wouldn't be looking so surprised."

Mr Wells, a little relieved by this distraction from defending his honour replied, "I brought you both here because of the anomaly."

"Do you mean the effect that caused us to pass through from your world to this?" I said, "Or do you mean the fact that apart from Mrs Wells, no one could see or hear us?"

"Neither. Though I believe they are both symptoms of the same phenomenon. I came here yesterday to see if the time cavern was still there."

"And why would you want to go to the time cavern?" said James sitting forward in his chair.

"There was a shift in time about two weeks ago. The thirteenth of March."

James, from habit, instantly removed his phone from his pocket.

"Let's check if there was any record of strange events. Damn, forgot, no internet."

"Mr Urquhart!" exclaimed Mrs Wells, "Control your language."

"Sorry."

"What made you think time had shifted?" I said to Mr Wells.

"The world changed to the one you see here."

"What do you mean?"

"There are hundreds of fractures. People everywhere have drifted across time Some are unware of..." said Wells.

"Do you mean," I said, interrupting him, "like those people who could not see us in the church?"

"You were seeing across time, I think. But some like me can remember their previous time line."

"And no one noticed except you, I suppose?" said James.

"And Mrs Wells?" I suggested.

"Yes. But she's come from a different world where she was

41

married to another me."

How many worlds are there, I wondered, not for the first time.

"Actually," he continued, "Someone on my world did notice or thought they did."

"Who?" said James. But Mr Wells continued to answer in his usual oblique way.

"Three days ago, I had an appointment in London for a meeting on my latest novel."

"The Time Machine?" said James.

"Yes. I had already published a version in serial form earlier this year for the Pall Mall. However, an American company wishes me to publish it as a book."

"Do they and your book exist in this world?" said James interrupting again.

"Yes, they do, but…"

"How did you get up to London from here?"

"By electric tram on Stane Street."

"Stane Street. You mean the Roman road?" exclaimed James.

"Yes. You should know all the roman roads still exist here. They are now major highways and fitted with tram rails. It takes only half an hour from Chichester to London."

"Are you saying the Romans never left Britain?" said James

"In this world, their empire still exists with their capital in Constantinople."

"So, all roads don't lead to Rome."

"Oh yes, they do. The capital can only be reached by ship."

There was no stopping James once he started an enquiry.

"What happened to the Saxons? Everyone seems to speak English."

"They were defeated by the great general, Ambrosius Aurelius, who in return for peace offered them the chance to join the empire."

"I thought it was Arthur?"

"Do you not mean Ursa? For Ambrosius was built like a bear."

I saw his puzzled look and said, gently, "Ursa is Latin for bear, James."

"Ah! Like the constellation, Ursa Major, the Great Bear?"

"Yes." I said.

"Gosh Elizabeth. I'm always surprised how much Latin I didn't know I knew."

I have noticed in James' world that impatience is often a prerequisite to the acquisition of knowledge and is gained by short and sharp questions and answers. Preambles are rare and usually met with frustration if not annoyance as I noticed with James here. However, I realised that we would only make progress by allowing Mr Wells to recount his story in his own way.

I said, "Thank you Mr Wells. That is most enlightening, but prey continue with your visit to London."

"While discussing my views on time travel with their representative," continued Wells, "he drew my attention to an article of the 13th of March in the New York Herald concerning a Mr Tesla who while experimenting with electro-magnetism received an injurious shock from the apparatus which he claimed allowed him to move a little into the past or future."

"What did he see?" said James.

"That is all that was reported but the article did recount that his laboratory was destroyed by fire on the same day."

"Very convenient, don't you think? All the evidence gone up in a puff of smoke."

"I am of the opinion that the fire was a direct consequence of his attempt to time travel."

43

"You mean he was trying to conduct an experiment on time and in the process shifted our world?" I said.

"Or," said James, "he was doing one of his mad electromagnetic experiments which caused an unintentional time shift and destroyed the building at the same time."

"Why do you think that?" I said.

"From what I can remember he was obsessed with telegraphy and the transmission of voice or pictures by electromagnetic fields. He thought the bigger the magnetic field he created the further he could communicate. He was so famous for this that they named the unit of magnetic field strength after him. He wasn't happy unless he'd managed to generate at least a million volts in his lab. I'm not surprised he blew it up. Possibly created a massive air discharge and in the process managed to distort the fabric of time and space."

"Was he killed?" I said.

"No." replied Mr Wells, "According to the article of the fire, he received just a few burns."

"And I think he carried on doing this stuff for decades." said James, "One thing though. I remember reading some article by him on how he might use a massive electromagnetic beam to communicate with Mars."

"Mars! You mean the Martians?" I said incredulously. "Did he succeed?"

"No idea. What do you think, Wells? You know them quite well."

Chapter Five

J.

I've never quite understood Wells' relationship with the Martians. I believe it began with the rescue of one which fell from the sky and had been shot by a clergyman. I think he wrote a story about it in this year, 1895, and called it 'The Wonderful Visit'. The trouble with Wells is that it's almost impossible to get a straight story out of him. A simple question like 'When did you first meet the Martians?' doesn't work. He must be manoeuvred into a position so he has to give you the fact you want. Nevertheless, I decided to have another go. Except Mrs Wells got in first.

"Herbert! Or whoever you may be. Am I now to believe you are from another world like me but on that world, we were never married?"

Ah. Progress.

"That is correct, Isabel. And I apologise for not marrying you."

She ignored his apology.

"And you have never had a relationship with Catherine Robbins?"

"I can assure you I have not and furthermore I have never heard of her."

She looked at me and Elizabeth and seeing no support said almost dejectedly. "Then in the absence of any sense or evidence to the contrary I must accept what you have said."

Then just as I thought we had we had resolved the matrimonial issue she turned to us and said, "But what has happened to the husband I brought here?"

I must admit what with being kicked out of time again my patience was running thin and said, "I imagine he's absconded with that Catherine."

Elizabeth grabbed me quite forcibly by the upper arm. "James! How could you say such a thing to this poor woman?"

"Where else could he be? This definitely is the year he ran off with her. So why not now?"

"But that is only conjecture. He could have left on an errand and on return failed to find his wife and is about the town looking for her."

There are times when I believe women abandon all sense, despite the facts presented to them, and will defend the impossible to defeat the obvious. I remember suggesting this to Elizabeth during a small discussion over the size of her wardrobe and how she never throws things away. She verified my conjecture by immediately reminding me of a number of occasions where she thought I did the same. I should record that although our garage is a little untidy, all its contents are essential. This has been proved often enough when I have been forced to consign things to the bin, that on questioning I could not think of a use, only to find they were needed the next day!

Anyway, Wells seemed visibly relaxed after his 'wife' acknowledged his version of events, so I took the opportunity to get some information on what the hell was going on.

"Did Tesla manage to build a device with enough strength to reach Mars?"

As I hoped, Wells grasped the opportunity to change the subject and said, "The day before the anomaly, while still in my own world, I experienced one of my out-of-time phenomena in which one of the Martian creatures visited and, through a trance, described a near future where my world would be transformed and contact lost between Mars and Earth."

If I didn't know him I would have guessed he was

recounting an experience from a séance. An event in another time-world he would attend often after the first world war in attempt to contact his dead son.

"So, what did they want you to do?" I said.

"A scene appeared showing you and your wife on a riverbank with me, and then at the church at Midhurst."

"With you?" I said.

"Yes! I did not understand at first but after the anomaly when I found myself in this world, I took the vision as a sign that we should meet. I recognised the River Rother and by its meandering path the place of rendezvous must be somewhere upstream from Midhurst. I immediately hired a launch to find you."

"And pray tell us, Mr Wells, what do you expect us to do?" said Elizabeth.

"I do not know. I presume to return us to our world and join with Mars."

"Thanks very much." I said. "So, all we have to do is join up space and time again and return us all to our own worlds. No problem, eh, Elizabeth?"

E.

I had now abandoned any attempt to make sense of anything as I was convinced Mr Sensibility had either packed his bags and taken a short holiday or had retired to a sanatorium for his health.

It seems we had been brought here to solve the conundrum of a rift between Mars and Earth but in the process slid into a different world and met Mr Wells' 'wife' whom he said he had never married. What were we supposed to do? I appealed to James for help, "Forgive me. But I cannot remember how or when we acquired the skills to assist Mr Wells in solving this puzzle."

"Nor can I." He said, looking as confused as me. "However, I do remember that in all our so-called adventures the prerequisite was that we didn't have a blooming clue what was going on."

I could not but agree and not for the first time wondered how we had survived so much together. However, his comment provoked a thought which although I did not want to pursue required explanation. I said, "You remember we discussed how there might be many copies of us in different worlds existing at the same time?"

"Yeah! Quite mind blowing," he said, using a quite colourful and I thought, quite accurate vernacular phrase.

"Then perhaps," I continued, a little hesitantly, "Perhaps on each adventure we have taken the place of the James and Elizabeth who did know what they were doing."

He turned to me looking a little stunned and holding my hand which I took at first as a sign for support rather than affection. "Elizabeth! How do you do it? You know that logical deduction would explain everything. Except...."

"Except what?"

"Why do we keep getting chosen instead?"

Mr Wells, whom I discovered could hold an argument and listen to us at the same time, said, "You must not worry about that. Because as you can move out of time there is only one pair of you. And before you ask, believe me, the Martians have looked."

I was much relieved by this and so was James although I could see, as a man, he regarded Mr Wells' last comment as a slight on his character. He was still holding my hand and said to me, "With hindsight, do you think we could have done better?"

"With hindsight, I should have taken up that offer you once

made to hide and live under the stairs. However, we are here and as usual we must make our own luck."

"Then," he sighed, "I think we need to find some information on the machine Tesla was working on when his lab caught fire. But first I'm starving and second, as we're stuck here, we need to find somewhere to stay and I think I know where."

He turned to Mrs Wells, "Is the Spread Eagle Hotel still here?"

I saw immediately his plan, for if it still existed then possibly the passage to the time cavern was there as well. And from there we might find our way home.

Mrs Wells replied, "Why yes. But it is a strange building, half-timbered and out of character with its surrounds. It is not very popular as it serves only English food. But I hear it is comfortable enough for travellers. But you can stay here for I have a spare room though the bed is a little small."

I immediately thanked her but said we did not want to impose and would prefer our own surrounds.

"Very well, if you wish. It is but twenty minutes by foot or you may take a tram which stops outside."

She then turned to Mr Wells. "Do you wish to stay here? I can prepare a supper."

"Thank you, I will take up the offer of the supper but I have already arranged lodgings at the Angel."

We took the tram to the hotel. It had not changed although it looked out of place amongst the whitewashed Roman buildings around it. But I was glad. An island, I hoped, of tranquillity in this sea of madness. At the reception, James thought it best if he took the lead in making a reservation as we had not seen any evidence of equality between the sexes here. I agreed, as a lady in my time paying for a room on behalf of gentleman could lead to speculation on her reputation, if not her occupation.

We were much relieved to discover the White Room was available and even more so when we found the passage door was still there in the chamber.

J.

The room was clean and, in this world, decorated in the style of a kind of oriental Art Deco. The walls were garden green and painted with trailing vines and cherry blossom. The windows, however, were still leaded glass. Against the far wall was a polished, sandy coloured, wooden double bed and I walked over to it and tried it out.

"Mmh. Nice and soft," I said, giving it a couple of bounces. "And very quiet. Do you want to try it out?"

"I think we should get some food first for if I lay on it now I would fall asleep in seconds."

I looked at my watch, "OK, Its four thirty. Let's see what they've got to eat."

Unfortunately, dinner wasn't served until seven so we demolished the remainder of my pie from the picnic.

"Ah. That's better," I said wiping the last crumbs of suet pastry off the pie dish with my finger. "Well, we've got a couple of hours to kill. I'd like to go to the library and find out what they know about Tesla."

"But it is Sunday."

"Perhaps they have different rules here. Let's have a look."

We eventually found the library on a dirt track called Knockhundred Row. It wasn't quite what I expected. It must have been about five-hundred years old and built in the old Sussex style. A few other cottages adjacent to it were built in the same way.

We climbed up the stone steps to a dark wooden door. A small paper sign pinned to the frame disclosed that it was open from two to six thirty on Sundays for a gardening club. I lifted the latch and slowly pushed the door open. Inside it smelt of books, dust, pipe smoke and varnished floorboards. In the dim light of the lattice sash windows were several gentlemen quietly reading the newspapers. There was no evidence of a gardening club meeting.

When I commented on this, she said, "I imagine it is a bolt hole for husbands to escape from the matrimonial home for a couple of hours."

"Really! You are such a cynic."

"And what about you?"

"You leave my attic alone." I said, pretending to be hurt, "I do very important work up there."

We tiptoed quietly across the creaking floorboards like a pair of elephants shod in iron shoes accompanied by the odd loud 'Shh!' emanating from behind the newspapers.

I got the distinct impression, judging by the raised eyebrows directed at Elizabeth, that females were expected to be at home 'managing' the family on Sundays.

We eventually found the science section after Elizabeth reminded me that in the nineteenth century it was called Natural Philosophy. It contained the usual collection of long forgotten books you find in an old second-hand book shop, except most of them were almost brand new. I wondered how much I'd get for some of them on Ebay in that condition.

"What exactly are we looking for?" whispered Elizabeth as we carried a pile of encyclopaedias and a thick dog-eared book called the Wonders of Science over to a table.

"We need to get a description of Tesla's equipment or at least some drawings or diagrams of the apparatus he was making when the lab caught fire."

"Do you really think the experiment he was doing caused time to shift?"

"I don't know. He was trying to do long distance telegraphy using massive EM pulses. He was using what we called in my day, a resonance oscillator"

"And do you think he was trying to communicate with Mars?"

"If he was I reckon he needed over a hundred million volts to do it."

"But is that not dangerous?"

"Yep. So we need to find out what he did to control it."

We searched for about an hour with no results. Then a loud jangling bell rang making us nearly jump out of our skins. I turned around to see a thin, geriatric man in a frock coat with a hand bell. He carried on making the racket until he was convinced all the gentlemen languishing underneath their newspapers had begun to rise out of their comfy armchairs.

"Damn! Looks like they're closing, and we've found nothing on him."

But just as I was giving up, Elizabeth said, "Here's a cutting from the New York Times about Mr Tesla. When is it?... Oh... 9th July 1891. He claims he has built a machine for making illumination. Does this help?"

I had a quick glance. It was a small faded brown article about Tesla making an illuminated light. I was about to put it down when I noticed the journalist had described Tesla's coil in the last paragraphs.

"It's a Tesla coil!" I shouted, catching the attention of the whole library. "Well spotted! Where did you find it?"

"It fell out of this periodical."

I had a look at it. "Oh, it's the Observatory Magazine! And from 1892! I'd like to sell this on Ebay."

"Is it famous in your time?"

"Only with sad idiots like me. It's one of the early publishers of articles from the British Astronomical Association. Let's see, who's the editor?" I turned to the inside cover. "Ah! Maunder. I think he was one of the opponents to Lowell's canals of Mars. Didn't believe they existed. How little he knew."

"So how does it work?" she said.

"What works?" I said, scanning through the articles.

"Mr Tesla's apparatus! James, concentrate! We are about to be thrown out!" she hissed in my ear.

"Oh yes. Sorry."

I read through the article quickly. "It's written by a journalist but there's enough here."

"Yes, yes, but how does it work?" she repeated impatiently.

"It's quite simple, really. We need a high voltage supply connected to a transformer that'll knock it up to a few thousand volts. Then put a thick coil across it and a few capacitors in parallel. Here's the clever bit. Put a break in the circuit and the capacitor will charge up until the voltage is so great a spark fires across the gap, then a current flows passing through the coil generating an oscillating magnetic field."

"And that will change the world?"

"Oh no. We need a much bigger voltage. We need a second coil with hundreds of loops near the first one which will detect the field from the primary coil. And this will build a massive charge. Tesla reckons he could generate millions of volts and produce a massive pulsating arc."

"And will that suffice?"

"I don't know. But I think this is what Tesla was trying to do when it blew up and the lab caught fire."

"And you really want to repeat the experiment? I was hoping to have a reasonable number of years of married life."

"So was I but do you have any better ideas?"

"I confess I do not."

By now most of the gentleman were beginning to stir and some were casting eyes rather disapprovingly in our direction. No doubt we had rather spoilt their afternoon snooze.

I whispered, "The difficult bit is getting a voltage supply and capacitors. I could try and make some Leyden jars for the capacitors."

"Leyden jars, James?" she exclaimed, attracting I think two 'Sshs' and an 'hurumph'.

"Yes. You get a...."

"Oh, I've made dozens of those."

"What?" I said falling back in my seat accompanied by another loud 'Shh!' from behind.

"They are very easy to make. Just jam jars, tin foil and a few nails"

Seeing my confused expression, she whispered "You have heard of Mary Shelley and her Monster?"

Yes. Why?"

"When I was at a Girton I joined a science club."

"I see." Nudging her gently, "Any excuse to meet men unchaperoned, I suppose."

"James! What a suggestion!" she whispered pretending to be shocked. "The farthest thing from my mind. I hope you are not implying I would become infatuated with scientists, are you?"

"Of course not. Dead boring lot. Always playing with electrical stuff and dead animals. Not the slightest interest in girls."

"Precisely."

"Unless you turned up, of course." I said, "How old were you? Nineteen?"

"A lady does not discuss her age."

I drifted off a little. "Mmh! Imagine you turning up in my lab when I was a student. That powder blue embroidered dress you wore when you first came to my house and that little hat with wild flowers. I would have..."

"James! Escape from your reverie and let me return to my subject."

I gave her my interested face while I continued with my dream. See, men can multi-task.

"That's better. Now listen, we thought we would try and emulate the creation of her monster."

"Did you know I used to think Frankenstein was the monster?" Still only half listening.

"Actually, I must confess, so did I. Now stop distracting me! We tried to bring an animal back to life. For this purpose, the club had borrowed a Whimhurst machine from the Cavendish."

"A what?" I said.

"A Whimhurst machine. To produce large galvanic .... Have you not heard of it?"

"Hey! I'm supposed to be the Science lecturer. You're supposed to be a lady of leisure."

"A lady of leisure needs to be fully occupied if she is to be a subject of interest in her society." Then she came up close to me and quickly whispered, "Not to mention of interest to a man she might wish to marry."

"Did it work?"

"I think he is standing here."

"What? Eh? No. I mean did you bring something back to life?"

"Two charcoaled mice and a pigeon which exploded covering us in feathers. I must admit there was some hilarity."

"In that case that qualifies you to be my assistant in this experiment."

"But we failed."

"Yes. But you qualify for finding it funny. We'll need some humour for this job. Though don't tell the Electrocuting Furry Animals Ethics Committee about your experiment when we get back."

After reading through the article for a third time I realised I wasn't going to keep it in my head. I said, "Oh, for a photocopier. I can't remember all of this."

"But you have your phone. You can take photographs."

"Of course! I hate you. Smart arse."

"Ssh!" came from the nearest old codger.

"I hope that gentleman there did not hear your comment."

"I think he did by the way he's looking at your rear."

"James!" And she immediately stood up from bending over the desk and smoothed her skirt.

I quickly photographed the article including a refresher I found on electromagnetism.

"Right. I've got what we need, I think. Now let's get some food. I'm really hungry."

"And so am I. May we eat at the inn for my feet in these shoes are bruised from walking?"

"Good idea. It's just around the corner. And I hope they don't dress for dinner as all we've got are the clothes we are standing in."

Just then the ancient with the hand-bell approached us, shook the bell, nearly deafening us and pointed at the door. With several apologies, we quietly tiptoed out in the same manner we came in.

The dinner was bangers, mash and gravy. It went down well. However, the beer was bitter and there was no tea or coffee. There was, however, an abundance of fruit juices which you could lace with gin.

After we had finished and were sipping a nice cold gin-soaked, crushed apple juice by the light of a single candle, I said, "Do you remember the first time we came here?"

"Yes. You seduced me and took me to bed." She said with a devilish smile and running her shoeless foot slowly up and down my leg.

"Oh! That is so not true. I offered to sleep on the couch."

"And you spied on me in my undergarments via the mirror there."

"Yes, it was fortuitously positioned, wasn't it?" I said savouring its memory.

"You were calculating the angles of incidence and reflection of the light while I was out of the room."

"And then you asked me to come to bed."

"Only because it was cold and I needed warmth."

Before I could respond she held my hand and looking at me with those eyes she gave me when we first met.

"And very warm you were too. Now, it is getting late. Shall we retire and perhaps you can find another distraction to take our minds off this adventure?"

I didn't need telling twice.

E.

The next morning during breakfast we discussed our plans for the day. James insisted his priority was to exchange his breeches for trousers. As I had now been wearing the same clothes for two days I acquiesced, and we went to town to replenish our clothes with Mr Wells' monies.

As we returned to the inn I told James that I still had reservations with regard to his dangerous scheme to build this infernal device and suggested perhaps we should first visit the time cavern to ascertain whether we might find a way home from there.

To my surprise, he quickly agreed and on being questioned he confessed that he was not looking forward to making Mr Tesla's device and maybe the time cavern was a safer option.

When we returned to our room and tried the old door to the passage I was gratified to find that it had not been opened for a long time, judging by the amount of dust that fell from the joints. However, we were disappointed to find inside that there was no means of illumination. We hunted around the room for a torch or candles but found none.

"I'll pop down to the reception and see if I can get something." James said.

And before I could protest, I found myself alone in the room with the open door to the tunnel. I quickly closed it and ran over to the chamber door. After what seemed ages, there was a knock on the door, and I heard James' voice call me. I quickly let him in.

"I couldn't find any matches, but I borrowed this."

To my surprise he produced a small bicycle lamp.

"Where did you get it?"

"It was attached to an old bicycle in the pantry adjacent to the hotel kitchen."

"You have stolen it, James?"

"Temporarily borrowed. Ill return it when we get back."

In any other circumstance, I would have admonished him severely for stealing but I confess the yearning to return home overrode my morals.

Instead, I said, "Does it work?"

"Of course." And he flashed a weak beam at the ceiling. Its strength was not reassuring. "Shall we go?"

And so, hand in hand, we opened the passage door and descended carefully in the dim yellow light of the bicycle lamp.

After about a hundred yards we came reassuringly to the vestry door.

"Let's go in and see if there are any candles on that altar again."

He tried the latch and with a creak the door opened and in we went. The altar was still there though it looked more like a Roman sarcophagus. On top was a candelabra with seven candles. Luckily, I did not have to prevent James 'borrowing' them, as on the floor in the far corner was an open box of spare candles from which we 'borrowed' half a dozen each instead. I was at a loss as to what we would light them with but I had learnt to appreciate from past adventures James' dictum that 'You can never have enough candles.'

We returned to the passage and continued until we came to the door of the time cavern. It was already open and there as should have been expected, in hindsight, was Mr Wells.

Chapter Six

J,

Wells was bent over the Mars globe. He always seemed to be one jump ahead.

"Good Morning, Wells." I said, "Fancy seeing you here. How is Mrs Wells?"

"She is as well as can be expected." He replied, still playing with the Mars globe.

"Where is she?"

"She has gone into town looking for her husband."

"Didn't trust you, eh?"

"I would prefer it if you did not find our predicament a source of amusement."

Poor old Wells. I hadn't realised how important she was to him.

"Sorry," I said. "If it's any consolation we know what you feel like."

"I don't think you do." He replied tersely, still examining the globe.

I ignored that and said, "So, what are you doing here?"

"I might ask the same of you."

"That's easy. We want to go home."

"I'm afraid that will be a little difficult. The machine as far as I am aware does not cross timelines. It only travels to the past and future."

"Then perhaps we can go home here. It's worth a look. Might find the future here is better than our world. What do you think, Elizabeth?"

"I was very happy where we were. We have friends and a nice home. I do not wish to rebuild another life which might not provide the same luck that we have had."

"Ok." I sighed, "Then that brings us back to plan A; attempt to reconstruct Mr Tesla's coil."

"Before you do that you might wish to look at this globe."

We both went over to him and the Martian globe.

"What do you see?"

I examined the planet. "Nothing. Just the red planet."

"Exactly! There is nothing there. It is completely blank."

I examined the surface. No indication of civilisation anywhere.

"What's happened?"

"I fear in this timeline the Martians may not exist or there is no communication with Mars."

"What does that mean?"

"It means we may not be able to rely on their skill to help us return."

"So, the only way is to build a Tesla Coil and try and reverse what Tesla did."

"How will you do that?" Elizabeth said.

"Good question."

I got out my phone and retrieved the photo of the article I'd got at the library on Tesla. It didn't look easy. I was going to need a lot of gear.

I said, "Where can I get things like wire, cables, insulators and jam jars?"

"You could try a local ironmonger," said Wells.

"Of course! Worth a try," I said, "Hope you've got lots of money, Wells. Let's see what I need."

I went through the article again.

"OK. We need at least ten jam jars for the Leyden capacitors you're going to make for me, Elizabeth."

"Ten!" she said.

"Yep. At least. With plastic lids."

61

"And if there is no plastic in this world?"

"Anything that isn't metallic. And, let me think, a box of six-inch nails and brass screws, a screwdriver, a hammer to bang in the nails, loads of tin foil, a few yards of thin copper piping and about - oh, I don't know - about 50 yards of insulated copper wire. And a wooden block and a round wooden post about three-foot-long and six inches in diameter."

"I now understand how your garage became the way it is."

"If my garage was here we wouldn't need to go shopping. Now what else? Oh, yes, and a high voltage power supply. And, since I'm a complete coward, a very long wooden stick to poke it with. I can't think of anything else. Can you?"

"How about some matches?" she said.

"What, to set light to it? That's a bit unfair; I'm trying to get you home."

"No, James, to light the candles after we have short-circuited the whole of Midhurst's electrical power supply and need to find our way out of here."

It was a good job someone remembered the important things.

E.

When Mr Wells and James entered the ironmongers, I was immediately treated to the spectacle of the antics of two small boys who have been let free in a toy shop without restraint. It was not without considerable effort that I managed to distract them from the gadgets and objects in what James described as an Aladdin's Cave of things he hadn't realised, he needed, and forcibly direct them to the items we required.

Eventually, after much discussion with the proprietor, which included a long discourse on the decline in quality of materials caused by the cheap imports of barbarian goods, we acquired the metals and woods for James' experiment. However, there then arose the question of their conveyance to the cavern for there was more than we could carry.

It was at this point that I must have succumbed to the beginnings of a brain fever for I found myself agreeing with James that an old rusty perambulator propped up against the corner of the shop would be adequate for our needs.

My illness did not become apparent, however, until while walking back along the main road pushing the perambulator, an elderly lady stopped us and berated my husband for buying his wife such a dilapidated carriage for our newborn child. James forgot himself and his manners and told her it was perfectly adequate and to mind her own business. An argument then ensued which drew in several other women who proceeded to discuss the frugality and selfishness of husbands and fathers. When, in the hope of ending this discussion, I protested that we did not have a baby, the women's attention turned to me and in a most unsavoury manner demanded to see the child to assess its welfare. Unfortunately, as James tried to manoeuvre the carriage around them to escape, a wheel fell off and, in the process, spilled the entire contents of the carriage onto the pavement.

There then followed a terrible commotion amongst the women as they tried in vain to recover the non-existent child from the materials strewn across the road.

It was at this moment that the brain fever must have taken fully hold for I fainted.

When I recovered, I found myself in bed with James by my side holding my hand and looking very apologetic. After some close questioning, coupled with a considerable amount of evasion by he whom I sometimes refer to as the love of my life, I discovered that after repairing the wheel they had placed me in the perambulator and pushed me back to the hotel.

The vision of the Squire of Hamgreen's daughter plonked in a small cart with legs and arms trailing akimbo, like an intoxicated doxy after a successful afternoon, and pushed in a cart through the streets of Midhurst in broad daylight by two men caused me, I am afraid to say, to faint again.

J.

I thought it best not to use in my defence that she was too heavy to lift and carry back to the hotel and that the pram seemed a good idea at the time. Nor to ask her to thank us for sacrificing all the equipment we had bought to bring her back to the hotel safely.

And certainly, not to mention that the wheel fell off again and that it required four strong men to lift the pram with her in it while we reattached the wheel.

In fact, I thought it best to stay very quiet, bring her lunch to the bedroom and sit in the corner studying intently the intricacies of nineteenth century wallpaper.

E.

I should record that I am normally of a reasonable and sound constitution and not prone to fainting fits, unlike some ladies I have known who have used it to their advantage with male companions or to escape from embarrassing situations. However, I can only say the state of unconsciousness saved me from a rather severe argument with Captain Dunderhead in which I may have used words which I later regretted!

J.

While I looked after Elizabeth, Wells took the pram to retrieve the equipment we had spilled and replenish the items that had been removed by the crowd. He then went to the chemist on north street and obtained a dozen empty green jars complete with cork stoppers.

When he returned to the inn, Elizabeth had sufficiently recovered to talk to me again on condition that the predicament with the pram, as she put it, was not recounted anywhere and certainly not to her father, her sister or her cousin Henry, on pain of a horrible death.

However, having retrieved all the items we still had to get it all to the cave. As we didn't want to go in via the church vestry we had to resort to bringing it all through the inn and up the passage. Elizabeth decided to stay in our room and refused to join us in this work on the grounds that having arrived at the inn in the form of a drunk strumpet in a cart and taken up to our room by one man, she did not want to be seen going up and down the stairs to the room accompanied by two men, even though one was her husband.

I decided not to mention that by staying in her room, while two men made a number of journeys up there, provoked quite a bit of interest amongst the clientele in the lounge.

Eventually, after several trips we got all the gear into the time cavern.

I checked all the equipment and was just about to pat myself on the back when I realised the most important item was missing: a high voltage power supply.

Wells came to our rescue by opening one of the consoles. "You should find adequate power in here. You may be able to connect your apparatus to this."

I looked inside and saw a row of junction boxes.

"How much power supply have we got here?" I asked, not really wanting to touch anything."

"I do not know."

"AC or DC?"

"All I know is that it provides some auxiliary power to the machine."

Oh, for a multimeter. I examined the junction boxes a little more closely and chose a pair of wires that didn't look like they could supply current for the whole of Midhurst.

"OK. It'll have to do." I said to no one in particular.

"Now for the Tesla coil. Let's start with the secondary coil. Pass that wooden post and I'll nail into this square stand like so. Now I'm going to carefully wrap this shellac coated wire around the post and hope it stays insulated."

The problem was I didn't have anything to hold it on the pole so as I wound it around the pole one way, it unwound itself.

"Should have bought some glue. Wells, if you hold it here I'll start winding."

After about fifty turns it held. "Good! This is going to take some time so Elizabeth, can you start making those Leyden jars. I think we will start with ten."

With Wells' help, she filled the jars with tin foil and wrapped a sheet of foil around each jar, while I continued to slowly wind the insulated wire around the post. Then I got the copper tubing and gently wound it around the post trying to make sure it didn't come into contact with itself along its entire length.

"Now we need the torus. We'll have to use the tin foil. I'll make a thick twisted roll of it and turn it into a doughnut."

Once I had managed to fashion the foil into roughly the right shape, I placed it carefully on top of the wooden post and connected one end of the secondary coil to it. The other end I connected to the nearest console in the hope it would act as an earth. I would dearly have loved to have had a multimeter to test the circuit.

When they had finished making the Leyden jars, I banged a nail into each of their cork lids so that they connected with the tin foil inside the jars. Then I joined up the nail terminals with a copper wire and another wire looped around the external tin foil of the jars to make ten capacitors in parallel. What the capacitance of all these jars was I had no idea. I attached a wire to the primary coil of copper pipe and the other end to the external foils of one the Leyden jars.

To make the spark gap I banged two nails about an inch apart into the wooden base and attached a wire to one of these nails and one of the nails in the lid of one of the Leyden jars.

"OK, now for the scary bit. I'm going to connect one wire from the console power supply hoping it's AC, to the primary circuit copper pipe and the second to one of the spark gap nails."

"James! Do you want to check the power supply is turned off?"

I felt a small bead of sweat form on my forehead. I looked at the console. It was off. I then gingerly connected the wire to the nail.

I stood back and looked at my handiwork and hoped that it would never fall into the hands of my students who would no doubt demand less stringent criticism and marking of their experimental work from that point onwards.

"What do you think?" I said, reconnecting one of the wires which had fallen off.

"I am thinking," she said, "why am I allowing the idiot who bought the perambulator to build a machine to alter the fabric of time and space?"

"Because you have complete faith in him?"

"I hadn't realised the advancement of science was dependent on faith."

"Rubbish, the advancements have all been made by people not knowing what they were doing. Look at Fleming who discovered penicillin by accidentally leaving some mould on the window ledge. Or Kepler who made a mistake in his calculations of Mars' orbit then made another mistake which corrected the first one and gave the right answer."

"And you will be successful in a similar way?"

I looked back at the pile of wires, coils and jars. It didn't inspire confidence. However, after all this effort I wasn't going back.

After checking the connections one more time, I said, "Ok, it's ready... Now let's all move to the door." I then flicked the power supply switch and ran to the tunnel. We waited. Nothing happened. After about five minutes, I said, "I think I need to push the spark gap nails closer together.

As I went back to table to adjust them, Elizabeth shouted. "James! Stop! They might contain charge!"

I stopped just in time and retrieving the long pole proceeded to first switch off the power supply then bang the nails closer together. It was good to see my five years in research was being put to good use. For some reason, each time I hit it I closed my eyes. I presume this was my body's natural defence to shield me from either a massive electrocution or my own stupidity.

When I was satisfied that the gap was close enough (this just happened to coincide with the moment I broke the pole) I said, "Right, let's try again."

I switched on the power with the three-foot remains of the pole and ran back to the door. Again, nothing happened. My heart sank. Then suddenly a spark crossed the gap with a thwack. Then another and another until it was firing sparks at about five a second.

"Now what happens?" Elizabeth said.

"God knows. Wait."

So, we waited and waited. The sparks became faster and faster. Then I noticed Elizabeth's hair was rising and fanning out. The same was happening to Wells. I put my hand up to my head and heard my hair crackle and noticed the hands of my watch were turning. It was at that point I remembered Gauss's theory and the advantages of Faraday cages and wished I had thought to buy some metal chainmail suits and rubber boots for protection.

Elizabeth shouted through the noise, "What is happening to us?"

I yelled back, "The room is filling with charge!"

Wells shouted, "You must turn it off before we are electrocuted!"

"What, go back in there?" They both looked at me. "Ok. I'll have a go".

I picked up the broken pole and slowly entered the cavern, earnestly praying that the coil didn't use me to discharge its voltage. Then, my god! A massive flash of lightning shot across the room to the Martian globe and I was out of the room and running down the passage, followed by the other two. After about fifty yards we paused to catch our breaths. I noticed her hair, had subsided back to its usual resting position.

"What do we now?"

"You must turn it off."

I wasn't enjoying this 'you' bit.

I slowly returned down the passage followed at some distance by Wells and Elizabeth. The light around the door was a blue green flashing glow and the air was thick with the smell of ozone. I gingerly approached the door holding my stick in front of me. Then just as I was about to enter I suddenly remembered something about the conductivity of wood and the perils of holding a long pointy thing in the air during a lightning storm. I dropped it quickly.

The thunderous flashes and the smell of ozone became stronger. Nevertheless, I went up to the door and peered through.

A great arc of plasma emanating from the torus was playing on one of the consoles. Then another hit the gantry. More flashes of lightning shot from the torus until there were five continuous blue-white snakes of plasma playing around the room. I stood transfixed, not daring to move until suddenly I felt a tingling sensation in my arm which slowly gripped my arm tight. I thought I was having a seizure. I jumped back and fell straight into Elizabeth's arms. "Are you alright, James?"

"God, it's only your hand. I thought for a moment I'd been electrocuted!"

But before I could recover, all the lights went out. Only the plasma illuminated us like a strobe light. Our movements were caught in jerky images. For a moment, I felt we were actually in one of those early Frankenstein horror movies. All that was missing was a dead body rising from the table.

Just as suddenly, everything went black and silent. No bang, explosion or fire. Just quiet and total blackness.

Elizabeth was still holding my arm. I felt her breath on my neck. It was hot and rapid. "Where is your lamp?" she whispered.

I searched my pockets. Normal people put things in a pocket with one hand and retrieve it later with the same hand. If you are ambidextrous like me, you put things in your pocket with one hand and then later search for it with your other. What's worse, the other hand actually thinks it put it there! I eventually found it and switched it on. The weak beam traversed the room. The apparatus seemed to be all in one piece though the spark-gap nails had melted into stumps. I continued to sweep the beam around searching for any signs of damage. But when I pointed at the Mars globe, a flash of lightning from the torus suddenly struck it and knocked the torch out of my hand. How I didn't pass out I don't know for in the last light of the weak beam I'd seen a small cat or rabbit-like creature with gossamer wings sitting on the globe - a Martian!

Chapter Seven

E.

It took a little time to find each other in the pitch black when James dropped the torch. Luckily, one of us had remembered to bring some candles. And Mr Wells, who on occasion smoked a pipe, produced some matches.

Thus, by candle light we were able to see a little way along the passage down which we had retreated after James claimed he had seen a Martian.

We were not convinced by his vision as he was a little deranged after his experiment. Mr. Wells, who seemed more composed than we, offered to go back into the cavern. We did not argue with him but gave him a candle and watched him walk back towards the cavern. This did nothing to help steady our nerves for his shadow playing on the walls gave the impression of another being and I expected any moment to see a Martian hovering before us. He soon vanished through the door to the cavern. We waited with bated breath. There was no sound and more disconcertingly, he did not return.

"Do you think we should follow?"

James didn't answer. In the pale candle light, I saw his hands were trembling a little and his face was deathly pale. I pulled him to me for comfort. Tiny sparks of electricity leapt from our clothes as we touched.

"Are you alright?"

"I think so. I keep on imagining those lightning bolts striking me." Then he regarded me quite closely, puzzled. "Your hair, Elizabeth."

"What of it?" I said. I put my hand to my head. I felt my hair crackle and adhere to my fingers.

"I presume by your look I am not presentable for receiving

73

guests?"

"Just, try not to touch any metal objects for a while. I think we're still highly charged."

"Do you think you really saw a Martian?"

"Yes. Or a creature like it. It was sitting on the globe. And to answer your question - yes. We should go and see what he is up to."

J.

As we approached the door, he came out.

"What did you see?" I said, hoping the creature was a figment of my imagination generated by the highly charged static in the cavern.

He turned and carefully closed the door. Then he whispered, "There are Martians in there."

The plural didn't escape me.

"How many? I only saw one before I dropped the torch." I whispered.

"There were at least three."

"At least?"

"The shadows from the candle made it difficult to see them."

"Did they contact you?" said Elizabeth.

He hesitated then said, "I felt a communication."

"Come on! Talk straight for once. Where did they come from?"

"They came here because they picked up the signal from your apparatus."

"Really?"

"Yes, and it has set up a portal between here and Mars."

"You mean we or they can travel between here and Mars?"

"It would seem so."

Elizabeth brought us back. "Never mind those creatures. Has your infernal machine caused the world to change? Are we back in our time?"

"No idea." I said. "I reckon we have two choices. One: go back and see what the Martians are up to and how they got here or two: run away. I'd like to opt for the second one. All we know is we're in a passage. We have no idea what's outside."

"And we have only these candles for light. Unless you want to go back into the cavern and retrieve your torch," she said.

My look gave her my answer.

"Then I suggest," she said, "we use what is left of these candles to our advantage and return to the world above and whatever it holds for us, or at least to the Vestry to borrow more candles.'

There was no arguing with that. We returned quietly up the passage leaving the Martians behind. Though on several occasions we did look behind to see if they were following us.

E.

We eventually arrived at the vestry door. After spying through the latch hole to ascertain no one was in sight we quietly opened the door and all three of us entered. My heart sank. It was as we had left it, including an absence of the few candles we had borrowed. My fears were finally confirmed that the experiment had failed when we entered the nave and found the same Romanesque windows and star studded ceiling.

Without any exchange of words, we moved as one to a pew and sat down.

It was getting late in the evening, and the great hall was lit by only half a dozen electric lamps. In their weak glow the pillars cast long dark shadows across the floor. It took me a few minutes to summon up sufficient energy to bring my thoughts back into focus. Mr Wells was writing in his notebook and poor James was looking dejectedly at the floor. I tried once again to recount silently to myself the events of the past two days. There were many unexplained gaps which I eventually realised all pointed to the person in the blue jacket as their source. I turned to him.

"Mr Wells, I need to ask you some questions." I said.

"Please do." He said, still writing notes.

"Good luck," said James with his head buried between his knees.

"When you arrived at the river were we not already in this world?"

"Yes."

"And pray tell me from where had you come?"

"Why, Midhurst, at the Angel."

"And were you staying there when the Martians informed you of the world change?"

"No. I was staying at my grandparent's hostelry at the Unicorn in Chichester."

James awoke from his despondency. "Isn't that pub supposed to be haunted?"

"I have heard such stories from my father. He told me of ghostly apparitions. One was of a Roman soldier."

"Not surprising being on top of a Roman city. Made a good story I presume to attract the locals. Sorry, Elizabeth, I interrupted. What did you do next?"

I was gratified to see a glimmer of enthusiasm from James. Mr Wells continued.

"When the world changed, I took a cab and tram to Midhurst and lodged at the Angel, from whence I hired the launch to find you."

"You were lucky finding us there, weren't you?" said James suspiciously.

"I did not know when you would appear. I travelled up and down the river for almost two weeks before I found you."

"But I thought you said you went up to London to see your publisher. You could have missed us." James said, now awakening a little.

"That only occupied a morning via the express on Stane Street. They were most insistent that I went. It was a risk but as it turned out quite fortuitous."

"Quite some risk."

"They were very persuasive."

"How?"

"They said they had information on a person who had time travelled and wished to know my view on it. I thought it might have been about you."

"Us?"

"Remember, I had been asked to find you. I thought it might be a clue to your whereabouts. There are not many people whom I know who can travel across time. It seemed too much of a coincidence to reject."

I said, "Perhaps the Martians wanted you to obtain information on Mr Tesla's accident."

"Afterwards the thought occurred to me also."

As I contemplated this, James said, "OK. I'll go along with that, but you said you borrowed clothes from Elizabeth's sister. Where or when was that?"

"I contacted her by telegram at Hamgreen, and she brought the…"

"You can talk to my sister Flory?" I interjected rather loudly; my voice unfortunately echoing off the walls and disturbing some parishioners whom I was glad to see could now hear us.

"Yes. By telegram"

"Why didn't you tell me?"

"You didn't ask."

The man is incorrigible! Our Mr Wells seems to be devoid of any social skills or empathy. Heaven help Isabella Wells if her husband is the same. I will remember to go easy on James next time wishes to give him a verbal lashing.

"How can I contact her?"

"At the Telegraph Office."

I turned to James. "We must go there now!"

James looked at his watch. "It's past midnight. It'll be closed."

He saw my impatience and said, "We'll go first thing in the morning. There's nothing we can do now."

"Just a minute. Is she of this world or ours?"

"She is of ours." said Wells, "It seems your home continues to have special qualities making it impervious, or resistant, to time."

"Then she is out of her time and alone! We must go to her!"

"We have to wait till the morning, Elizabeth. Even if we try to go there now, how are we going to get there? Do you think we'll get a cab or tram at this time of night?"

I turned to Mr Wells.

"I am afraid there is no transport at this time of night. You must wait until the morning."

I could see no argument with this and reluctantly returned to the Inn. I did not sleep well.

J.

Despite what I thought was the pressing need to get back to our world I felt that I wasn't going to get the full use of Elizabeth's faculties until we'd seen her sister. However, Wells insisted that we checked on Isabel before we went to

Hamgreen. I decided to let the two of them sort it out.

Elizabeth won and we were dragged off, almost running, to the Telegraph Office. After some heated discussion on what to say we managed to send a telegram. Then we waited and waited for a reply, while Elizabeth paced around the foyer. It was almost two minutes before the answer came.

'Am safe and well. Do come.'

Then we took the tram to Isabel Wells' house. It had started raining and it made the town look shabbier. Here and there coal smoke rose from chimneys.

When we got to the road where Isabel lived, I whispered to Elizabeth, "I hope she hasn't found the other Wells."

"My god! Supposing he's in the house!"

"Yeah. I don't want to see TWO sociopaths get in a fight."

"Maybe you should go in first," she suggested.

"Me?"

"No. You're right. Another man turning up may not help. I will do it."

When we arrived at the house we explained the situation and possible consequences to Wells who eventually understood enough to agree to Elizabeth's plan.

She knocked on the door and to our surprise an old lady dressed in black answered. I presumed it was Isabel's mother and I could see Elizabeth was having difficulty explaining her presence. Probably the woman was deaf as a post I thought. I was about to join Elizabeth when she came back looking flustered.

"What happened?" I said when she returned.

"She said she is the maid and told me Isabel is visiting a friend!"

"Did she say when she'd be back?"

"No. she does not know. But does not expect to see her until this evening."

"Then we must go into town to search for her," said Wells.

"I am not delaying seeing my sister. And who is to say she has gone to town?"

Elizabeth had that entrenched expression she used when nothing was going to persuade her from the path she'd chosen.

"Maybe we can persuade that old lady to leave a note for her." I said, hoping to calm things down a little.

"Yes! What should we write? Oh, I know, we will tell her if she turns up to come to my home."

Wells said, "I agree." And pulling out a note book, he scribbled Elizabeth's address on a page and was about to march off to the house when she grabbed him and said, "No, let me do it. I think you turning up may cause confusion."

And with that accomplished we walked down to the tram station in the rain to find a way to Elizabeth's home at Hamgreen.

E.

At Cocking, we alighted from the electric tram and enquired at a bakery, which seemed to be the only place with signs of life in the village, for a cab to take us to the Lodge at Hamgreen. The lady, who had the white powdery complexion of one exposed to a lifetime of flour, directed us to a young man dressed in dark green livery, fast asleep on a carriage under a tarpaulin to keep off the rain. James managed to wake him and explain our requirement. For some reason, he seemed reluctant and on further enquiry he said it was because it was outside the pale. What this meant I did not at first understand but I was pleased to see he eventually understood the generous offer for the fare and we clambered into the carriage while the man made a makeshift cover with the tarpaulin sheet to shelter us.

I expected him to retrieve horses from somewhere but instead he climbed into the front seat and pulled a bronze lever. At first nothing happened. Then we heard a swooshing noise beneath us which gradually got faster until after about a minute it became a smooth hum.

James thought it might work on the principle of a Stirling engine though he could not ascertain the heat source.

Then with the pull of another lever, the carriage jolted forward on to the road, just missing the Midhurst Chichester tram which sounded its horn in annoyance several times. Our cabbie in reply made a number of gesticulations, despite the presence of a lady, which were more than obvious in their implication. I was about to admonish him but James stopped me as he worried I would not react well to receiving a similar response. When I suggested that I would expect him to defend my honour if such an event occurred, he said that judging by the girth and fitness of the cabbie, he might be unable to fulfil my expectations.

I should record that the attitude of men of his time in defending a woman's honour is sometimes difficult to understand. James says his philosophy is simple and follows Tacitus' dictum. I have to admit on occasion that running away to live another day has been the most appropriate option.

Just before the hill up to the Downs the cabbie turned the carriage left on to a straight chalk street and worked up to a speed of about fifteen miles an hour, which we all agreed, judging by the meandering of the carriage and the depth of the rifes either side, was more than adequate. The rain grew heavier and much time was spent trying to avoid water dripping or pouring through the various holes in the tarpaulin on to our clothes. To add to our misery the wind had risen and sudden squalls of rain would blow in from the sides just when we thought we had found a dry place to hide. On one occasion, I inadvertently pushed the slack tarpaulin roof up to relieve its pressure on my head from the accumulated water. Unfortunately, this caused a deluge of water to be released through a hole into James' lap. I confessed I had some sympathy with his short tirade on my temporary idiocy although his language could have been less anatomical. After a little further discussion involving slurs on our respective characters and tempers and trying to dry his wet trousers we eventually agreed it should not be brought up in conversation again.

During the temporary silence that followed, now and again through a gap in the tarpaulin I saw glimpses of the countryside. I was struck by the absence of woodland and it reminded me of eastern parts of Sussex which had been denuded of forests for the ships of the Napoleonic wars. We passed dozens of little fields bounded by small hedgerows, except in this world they were square or oblong and the tracks ran straight between hedgerow borders. In fact, I do not think we saw a bend in a road anywhere. James said it reminded him of a visit by a friend from the Americas who after travelling about twenty miles along the winding, twisting, main roads of Sussex suggested England could save a fortune in the import of motor fuel by just straightening out all the roads.

After about half an hour of some discomfort, and with water beginning to seep down my neck the carriage suddenly came to a halt and the driver pulled back the awning sufficiently to let us see his rain-soaked face and also, unfortunately, to let in the rain which by now was pouring down in buckets.

"The road ends here at the pale." He said. "This is as far as I go."

I looked out from under the tarpaulin and saw that the road and fields had abruptly stopped at a thirty-foot-high chalk and earthen wall stretching right and left into the distance behind which stood a dense fir tree forest.

James spoke to the driver, "We paid you to take us to Hamgreen."

"It's just down that track," he said, ignoring him and pointing at a gap in the wall into the forest.

"Why don't you carry on? Is it a magical forest full of strange beasts?"

"Do you take me for a primitive?"

"You tell me."

"Magic is for children."

"So what's the wall for?"

"Keep the wild life off the fields." He replied giving us a look indicating that that was the most obvious thing in the world. Then taking pity on us, he said, "Look. The cab can't travel on this track 'cos it'll break the under-carriage"

" But it's raining! We haven't got any coats!" James continued.

"This is as far as I go. If you want to change your mind, I'll take you back to Cocking. No extra charge."

"What do we do if we can't find it?"

"You will. Now make up your minds I have other customers waiting."

"Ok, take us back and we'll find someone who will." said James.

I immediately protested. "We cannot go back! I must see my sister."

"I'm not being abandoned in the middle of countryside I don't even know. We haven't even got a map."

I was saved from further argument by Mr Wells.

"Those telegraph wires," he said pointing at a line of

wooden poles along the road. "Do they go to Hamgreen?"

I looked to the side of the road and saw the wires disappear into the woods.

"Must do," said the driver, "There's no other place in the forest."

"Thank you. Then we will take your leave and follow them."

James shrugged. "Well, if you two want to try it, I suppose I'm coming."

Then with no more ado we decanted from the carriage into the rain.

We watched the cab turn and go back to Cocking and comfort. James said, "Come on then. Let's get in the woods. It'll be drier there until it stops raining."

We passed through the earthen wall towards the trees following the poles. Puddles were already forming. I was thankful we were wearing our walking boots although an umbrella would have been useful, for I was nearly soaked to the skin.

As we entered the wood I was immediately struck by its darkness. It felt quite eerie. This feeling was not helped by James who said, "This reminds me of Mirk Wood. I hope we don't meet any Orcs."

I started. "I thought you said Orcs weren't real."

"Not in my world. God knows what they've got here."

The thought of Orcs made me shudder a little for one of the first moving pictures James had shown me was entitled Lord of the Rings during which I spent much of the time during its performance hiding behind a cushion trying to believe that none of the creatures portrayed were real.

We followed the wires further into the forest. Thankfully they followed a wide track. James was holding me quite closely but I was not quite sure whether it was for his support or mine. He whispered, "The cabbie said the wall was to keep

84

out the wildlife. What do we really expect to meet in the woods in your time? Deer, boar, wolves?"

"In my world," I said, "I only ever saw deer and rabbits."

"Let's hope it's the same here."

As if to prove my point, three frightened roe deer followed by a stag suddenly emerged from the trees in front of us and ran across our path. I refrained once again from admonishing James on the language of his exclamation.

When he had recovered and let go of my arm, he said. "Sorry. I'm in a forest in a strange world, out of my depth and a bit stressed."

But before I could reply Mr Wells added to the situation in the way that only Mr Wells can. "There is something else to worry about."

"What's that?" said James.

"It has stopped raining."

We all looked up. It had.

"Isn't that a good thing?" said James.

"Possibly. But what is more," he continued, "there is no water dripping off the trees."

He was right! The wood was completely dry and very silent. Not a sound. It took a moment before I realised what he meant. It had not rained here. But it was James who realised the implication.

"Don't tell me we've passed through another damn portal?"

"It would seem so," said Mr Wells.

"God! What time or place are we in now? I bet that cabbie knew something. Should have asked him if he knew if anybody ever came back out of this wood."

Usually when one of us is at a loss the other is able to come up with a distraction but I could not but agree with his sentiments. It was so quiet you could hear our breathing and to compound our predicament it was getting darker. Seeing

85

no other choice, we decided to go onwards and follow the wires in the hope that they led to my home.

J.

After about a hundred yards it had become so dark we couldn't see the wires and had to rely on looking for the next telegraph pole. This involved one of us standing by a pole then the other two going off looking for the next one and keeping in sight of each. Any locals watching this would have thought we'd all escaped from the local sanatorium. Then suddenly a light appeared in the distance in front of us. I pointed it out and we all concluded, not just me I would like to emphasise, that it must be Hamgreen and like three moths we were off towards it, until we realised as it rose higher in the sky it was the moon.

We were now off the path and had not only lost the wire but any sign of any poles. We tried to retrace our steps which was quite difficult as although fir woods are virtually devoid of undergrowth, they look the same in any direction. Then just as we'd decided we were completely lost and would never be found, save as a pile of white bones and rags, Wells stopped us.

"Listen!" he whispered.

We listened and after a while I thought I heard a fluttering high above.

We strained our ears in the silence. Then again, the sound of something in the trees.

"It might be an owl." whispered Elizabeth.

"Or bats." I said.

"Thanks." She said, "First Orcs, now I have the thought of bats tangling in my hair."

"That's a myth," I said.

"I will be the judge of that."

Then a white shadow flew across the moon.

"Phew! It was only an owl."

But as we carried on along the track I was sure I could hear fluttering sound again in the trees.

Elizabeth whispered, "I think it is following us."

"No. I think it's just making sure we leave its territory. Birds are like that."

Then Wells, who obviously thought that just being lost in a dark wood in a different world was not sufficiently scary, said, "I think it could be a Martian."

"What makes you think that?"

"Look there." he pointed at a branch in front of us and for a moment before it vanished we saw a small white cat or rabbit-like creature with its shimmering gossamer wings.

We stood for a moment saying nothing then Elizabeth hissed, "There it is again! See about fifty yards down the track."

Wells whispered, "I think it might be fortuitous to follow it."

And before we could argue on the merits of following alien creatures in the middle of a dark wood, he started walking off in its direction.

With no poles or wires anywhere in sight to guide us we decided to go along with him.

But as we approached the creature it vanished again and reappeared another fifty yards down the track. After about the fourth appearance I was beginning to lose all hope when Elizabeth shouted. "There's the gate to the Lodge!"

And there, illuminated by the moon which shone through a gap in the trees, were two old stone gate posts straddling the track. I recognised them immediately. We passed through them out of the wood and on to a gravel drive and then half-walked, half-ran as fast as we could until we saw the lights of the Lodge come into view. By the time we reached it I was convinced that we'd made enough noise on the gravel to wake up the whole forest. It was gratifying to see Elizabeth's home again, not least because it seemed it hadn't changed since our last visit. There were the stone ashlar walls and the vines growing up around the windows up to the roof.

Elizabeth ran up to the door and pulled the bell loudly. Immediately the door opened and a young woman dressed in a knee length, black skirt and a green T-shirt opened the door.

"Hello, Elizabeth. You made it. Oh, hi, James and who's this? Mr Wells, isn't it? Come on in and have some tea."

It took us a moment to recognise Flory for she was dressed in the fashion of my era in what we had presumed was 1895.

Chapter Eight

E.

My mind was awash with confusion. I had left my sister in 1873. Twenty years had passed yet here she stood before us not a day older and in one of my modern dresses. There was only one question.

" Flory. When are we?"

"Why Elizabeth, we are in your time."

"Then we've got back to our world! Fantastic!" said James. Oh, the relief.

But then Flory said. "No. I mean 1895."

"What is the date?" said James.

"I believe it is Monday, the 25th of March."

"But why are you in that dress?" he said.

She drew her skirt closer to her and said rather defensively, "I have come to enjoy their comfort and when I am not receiving guests I relax in them. It is the Lycra; it is so forgiving. Is it not, Elizabeth?"

"Yes, I can't deny it," I said, "But how are you, I mean we, in this time?" for the hall still looked of my period with the pale green walls and old Georgian table except it was lit by electrical lamps.

"First things first." said Flory before I could comment further, "You must all change out of those damp clothes before you catch a chill. James, you can wear your gardening clothes our father borrowed. Mr Wells, I have nothing for your girth and I would suggest a dressing gown 'till we have dried your clothes.

"In the meantime Lilly will prepare some warm refreshments."

"Lilly, my maid, is here?" I exclaimed.

I must remember that Lilly's main skill is knowing everything about me and letting me know it. James, unfortunately, is aware of this and despite my efforts to keep them separate, if an opportunity arises to get my old maid on her own, he will immediately quiz her for any gems from my upbringing.

Flory said, "Oh yes. We are all here. By the by, I see you received the clothes I sent you, although James, I notice you are not wearing the breeches and mustard stockings. Did you not like them?

"The stockings didn't fit, I'm afraid."

"Pity. I was looking forward to seeing you in them. I thought you would look very fetching."

"Not as fetching as your legs which I see have the perfect shape of your sister's."

"It is not etiquette to comment on a lady's legs in her presence, Mr Urquhart," she said trying unsuccessfully to pull down her skirt.

"In my limited experience," he said, turning to me quickly to ascertain whether he was treading in dangerous water and then ignoring my affirmation that he was, "that's the best time to compliment a lady on her pins."

A lifetime of not showing a leg or ankle, let alone revealing one to a gentleman, is a habit hard to break. James knows I still feel uncomfortable with this although it does not dissuade him from drawing attention to mine when he thinks an opportunity arises. However, his comments in this direction are always difficult to counter for, as any girl with sense knows, a compliment regarding her form from someone she admires should not be rebuked.

Once we had changed, Flory said, "Now come into the parlour. I have a surprise for you."

We followed her into the parlour. On entering, the first thing I noticed was a strange typewriter with a bright red glowing light bulb next to the keyboard. The second and more important item was Isabel Wells standing next to the window.

J.

My first thought on seeing Mrs Wells was to wonder if she was the same one, we had met earlier, because by this time if someone told me I was in Timbuktu in a fairy dell on the other side of the Moon I'd have believed it.

Wells, in his usual non-passionate self, said on seeing her, "Oh, hello. How did you arrive here? Did you see our note?"

"What note, Herbert?" She said with equal passion and remained by the window. And they say romance is dead.

We then explained our plan to contact her which, to use Elizabeth's vernacular, she regarded us with not a little incredulity. When we'd finished, she said simply, "No. The reason I am here is that Miss Bicester and I," looking at Flory, "became acquainted at the library in Midhurst."

The coincidences were piling up again. We all immediately turned to Flory who told us to sit down. I flopped onto a sofa, exhausted, and Elizabeth joined me, wrapping her arms around my body and pressing her head against mine. She smelt deliciously of rain and new perfume. The Wells family however, decided to remain standing in their respective corners. Flory then told her story.

"I will start from the beginning when the anomaly occurred."

She sat down on a straight-backed chair and leaning forward, said in an almost confiding voice, "I did not notice a shift in time until the morning of the 13th March when I came down for breakfast. It was the electric lights which first drew my attention to it. Then I heard a bell in the parlour followed by a strange clattering sound. When I entered, I found it was that machine over there," pointing to the sideboard, "which had appeared out of nowhere.

"That red light was flashing and from out of the apparatus came a stream of white tape which on examination had typed writing on it. When it stopped, I laid it out on the table and I found it was a message from Mr Wells who said he had instructions to meet you both and could I bring clothes suitable for 1895 to the Coaching Inn at Midhurst. As I thought I was living in the 1870s I had no idea what was required! Nevertheless, I picked up some garments for Elizabeth then Smithers drove me in the carriage to Cocking to catch the Midhurst coach. My fears that time had changed were reinforced when I regarded the countryside and were confirmed when an electric tram appeared at Cocking.

I said, "That was brave of you, out on your own and in a different time."

"I did not find it easy but the need to find you outweighed my fear. Anyway, at Midhurst, I bought clothes for James then took them to the coaching inn where I gave them to Mr Wells. I was disappointed to find you were not there. Mr Wells could not tell me when or where you would arrive except that you would somehow appear on the river and for that reason he had hired a launch to look for you. I must admit I did not regard his plan with much hope. He was of the same opinion and after some discussion we eventually agreed that I should return home and wait for a message which would appear on that machine.

"For nearly two weeks Mr Wells sent me messages informing me that he had still not found you so yesterday I took it upon myself to return to Midhurst to help search for you."

"Did you not send Mr Wells a telegram that you intended to visit?" said Elizabeth, who by her warmth of her body against me told me she was nearly off to slumber land.

"I tried but I could not understand its operation. I went to the inn but Mr Wells was not there. Presuming he was on the river I filled my time with a visit to the library to try and ascertain from the periodicals what had happened, but to my surprise although everything was different there was no news of the change. In fact, apart from Mr Wells nobody else seemed to notice. It was there that I met Mrs Wells who was also examining the periodicals, and I gleaned during our conversation that she was suffering from the same experience as me but had lost her husband. When she informed me who she was I said I thought he was out on a launch. She then became rather agitated and to help I convinced her to tell me her story."

Isabel took over, "I described our meetings and Miss Bicester concluded that you, Mrs Urquhart, were her sister. We returned to the inn but Herbert was nowhere to be found. Miss Bicester then suggested that I return to her home where she concluded, quite rightly it seems, that your journeys would eventually involve a visit to her home."

"So," I said, "we are all here together and it seems no further forward. What do we do now?"

"We return to the cavern and build another coil." said Wells trying to unsuccessfully light a pipe with damp matches from his dressing gown, below which protruded two stockinged legs with suspenders.

"I'm not doing that again." I said with some force.

"Do you have any better ideas?" he said, still trying to light his pipe.

"Yes," said Elizabeth, raising herself from my body, "I suggest we all go to bed and have a good night's sleep after which we may find ourselves in a better position to discuss our problem. Is my bedroom available, Flory?"

"Yes. We prepared rooms in anticipation of your arrival. I will inform Lilly to provide some hot water."

She then turned to the Wells. "I hope you do not mind. It is a delicate matter. But are you to share a room or...?"

"Certainly not!" they both said in unison.

"I apologise. Please forgive me but I..."

"We are not married to each other." said Wells. "I will sleep on the sofa if you will bring me blanket or two."

And with that he plonked himself on the sofa and said, "Good night."

We all looked at him then Elizabeth turned to me, "Come on, James, get up and take me to bed before I drop asleep here and you have to carry me." And she pulled me reluctantly off the sofa.

E.

When I awoke, the sun was shining through the curtains and for a moment, as I gazed around my familiar room, I thought everything had been a dream. And thus, the presence of the man sprawled across my legs and snoring gently on my bed, dressed only in his underclothes, I confess, momentarily gave me quite a shock regarding my virtue.

As I tried to remove my legs from under him, his eyes opened and seeing me, he smiled and slowly crawled under the covers uninvited until he was nestled up beside me. We lay together for a while, wearing what little clothing we had not discarded, in our safe cocoon drifting in and out of sleep until a gentle knock at the door took us from our slumbers.

"Good morning, Lizzy and Mr Urquhart. I hope you slept well. Flory and the other guests are at breakfast."

"Thank you, Lilly. Tell them we will join them in a while." said James.

When she had left, he said, "God! I could sleep here all day."

I agreed but also reminded him we had agreed we would form a plan today.

"And that plan doesn't involve lying under the covers with you all day, I presume." he whispered.

"No, it doesn't," I said, carefully removing a hand which had somehow evaded my defences and found my breast.

His sister and I, on our occasional afternoon teas, while James was busy re-arranging the garden or 'working' in his attic, have often exchanged humorous anecdotes from our respective periods on the skills a lady needs to defend against 'wandering hands' so to speak and found, not surprisingly, much commonality. Jill told me once that she knew a cad who was referred to as 'The Octopus' on account that even if a lady held both his mischievous hands securely, she would still find her garments compromised. I replied that I believed that at every soiree I attended one would be found, and it was a duty to point such persons out to warn naïve debutantes.

But to return. We dressed and joined Flory and the Wells in the parlour where we spent over an hour recounting our experiences fortified by copious quantities of coffee, tea and toast. Eventually we all agreed, having verbally trodden over the paths to my home numerous times that the only solution to our predicament was to build a new machine and that the place of choice was the time cavern. There was however, as James reminded us, the question of the presence of the Martians.

Mr Wells led the discussion on this topic. "I think we must agree that the appearance of the Martians at the cavern and in the forest, confirms that Mr Urquhart's apparatus restored a link to Mars which allowed the creatures to transport themselves to our world. And the fact that one guided us to the Lodge suggests they are here to help us."

"But how do we contact them? They're elusive little beasts at the best of times. Never quite in or out of our world," said James, carefully applying the last morsel of confiture to his toast.

"That's easy." said Mr Wells.

"How?" I asked.

"There is one sitting on the mantelpiece."

We all turned around in shock and there it was! Then, as I regarded the small white creature, it caught my eye. Its wings shimmered and before I could resist, I felt my mind falling and spiralling into an abyss. Somewhere outside me I was vaguely aware of James holding my arm and his voice faintly calling me, but it was not enough.

After a moment, the room came back into view, but it was distorted in some way and out of focus. James and the others were but dark shadows, almost like smoke and growing smaller. Then I realised I was rising into the air. I passed through the ceiling of the parlour then my bedroom and the roof until I found myself suspended or floating high above my home. As I looked around me, I saw the great forest stretching to the horizon towards the east, but to the west it stopped along a straight line, beyond which were miles and miles of fields. Then I, or the countryside, began to slowly revolve and I felt myself gently pushed through the air by an invisible force. After a few moments, I had left the forest and as I floated across the landscape I saw for the first time the north of the country. Mr Wells was right. It was desolation itself punctuated by great factories belching clouds of white and brown smoke. Canals and railways criss-crossed the landscape. Between them wooden shanty towns of humanity to serve the great furnaces. I wondered whether they were slaves. Then I dived down to towards a village. As I got closer I recognised the church of Midhurst. It came towards me faster and faster. I expected to be impaled on the weather vane but instead I passed straight through it, through the nave and the earth below until I arrived in a dark cave.

I recognised the time cavern immediately for there was the Tesla coil. But it was not the one James had built. This was three times larger and beautifully designed as though made by a craftsman. Above it a large steel globe hung. But as I approached it the vision vanished and I found myself lying on a sofa with James by my side holding my hand and Flory and the Wells looking on.

J.

The Martian had gone. I laid her gently on the settee to check her breathing but before I could stop her, Flory had waved some smelling salts under Elizabeth's nose, which brought her quickly out of her trance.

"Thank god you're back," I said, feeling her forehead and checking her pulse. "Are you all right?"

"Yes. It was just one of those awful Martian nightmares."

"What do you think it told you?"

She recounted the dream.

"So, Wells is right. We have to make another Tesla coil."

"I do not think so. I believe the Martians have made one for us."

"Great. So, all I have to do is switch it on. Did I tell you that I wasn't into heroics or suffering an early death from electrocution?"

I looked around for support or sympathy and got none, save from Elizabeth.

Flory said, "Is it necessary for us all to go? Would it not be better for just one of us to go," looking at me, "and operate the machine to return us to our world."

So much for 'Over the top and we'll be right behind you.'

"What a good idea," I said, a bit angry, "I'm quite happy for you to go on your own."

There then followed some words from both sisters which I wish I hadn't started. Eventually it was agreed that we should all go as it was thought if we jumped into another world at least we would be all together.

The return journey to Cocking was a little more pleasant. I was volunteered to sit in the passenger seat next to Smethers. In the sunshine, the forest was quite a different place from the previous night and we passed through the Pale without incident.

When we got off the tram at Midhurst we went immediately to the nearest ironmongers and bought torches and spare batteries for everyone. At first, we thought we would go to the time tunnel via the vestry but I didn't trust the church to keep us in this world; so once again we entered by our room in the coaching inn. God knows what the proprietor and customers thought three women and two men were all doing up there.

We lit our torches and proceeded in single file down to the time cavern.

I opened the door very carefully. The air didn't smell of ozone anymore but I remained tense, expecting an electric shock at any moment. I shone my torch into the room and was amazed to see a state-of-the-art Tesla oscillator in the centre of the room. It was a masterpiece. The two coils were neatly wound and the Leyden jars had been replaced by large blue capacitors. My tin foil torus was replaced by a beautiful shiny steel one about three times the size. I noticed my apparatus was now a pile of junk by the console. When we were all in the room I said, "Any volunteers to switch it on?"

Surprisingly, no one moved so I went over to the console and pressed what was later to referred to in certain select circles as the red button.

Part II

The Space Between Time

Chapter Nine

E.

When I opened my eyes, I found myself floating on my back in a black firmament with the stars shining impossibly sharply around me. I kept perfectly still, not least because I was restrained by an invisible harness which tightly wrapped my body. There was no sense of motion. For a few moments my mind was blank, hypnotised by the view. Then I remembered. A silhouette of James upon the wall of the cavern when the bolt of lightning struck. Was I dead? Was he dead? The thoughts caused a cold clamminess to run down my back. In hope, I tried to turn my head, but I was constrained by some invisible force.

I closed my eyes again and tried to relax and think what I should say to my maker, for although I thought I had not lived a bad life, I knew it had not been entirely virtuous. Just when I had convinced myself that I might have to spend some time in purgatory, I felt something brush my face. I opened my eyes slowly expecting either an angel or devil and nearly jumped out of my skin for there was James' face grinning above me!

"Hooray! You're awake."

"I thought we had died!"

"Nope. Well, not yet. Though that flash of lightening was a bit of a shock."

"Where are we?"

"Don't know. First, let's get you out of these straps."

He pressed something on my breast and the invisible harness released me.

I moved my arms and legs and raised my head in relief. Then I felt his hands on my waist.

"Now, be careful," he said, "there is virtually no gravity here for some reason. Hold on to me."

As I tried to rise I began to float slowly float up into the air. He grabbed my flailing hand.

My stomach felt I was riding a charabanc.

"It's OK. Try and relax." His hand slowly ran up and down my body. Stroking me until a calm returned and I kissed him.

"How are you so relaxed?" I asked.

"I'm not. Seeing you in that state just made me forget about myself. No idea why." And he returned my kiss.

After a few moments when my nerves had calmed enough to allow me to think, I began to notice my surrounds. The view did not aid my constitution for there was no floor! We were suspended inside a sphere no more than fifty feet across whose boundary in all directions was formed by large lattice windows made of bronze or red gold through which the dark fields of stars shone. Except I had the distinct feeling that there was no glass and that we were looking directly into space. What held in the air in which we breathed I do not know.

Suddenly James appeared from nowhere and upside-down in front of me.

"This seems to be a ship although it may be a time machine." he said as my poor brain tried to assimilate his image. "I can't tell from those stars whether we're moving through space or time or both."

I slowly turned around. The chamber was quite empty apart from two large globes which I recognised immediately as Mars and Earth. They seemed to be suspended in the air.

"Where are the others?" I asked.

"I've no idea. One moment there was a flash, the next we were here."

But I wasn't listening for the stars which I thought had been safely held outside the sphere where moving and coming in through the lattice-work.

J.

At first I didn't realise what she was staring at. But as I turned around, I saw them. They were coming closer and closer. Tiny globes of orange, blue and white glowing lights.

"I don't know what's going on but I reckon we should try and avoid them."

"It's too late James! Look!"

I saw one then another pass through her. Then one emerged from my chest and into her body. I could literally see them pass through us.

"What are they doing?"

"I don't think they're doing anything. Can you feel them?"

"No. It is as if we are not here."

The light in the room changed and grew brighter and above us I saw a swirling galaxy rising and slowly moving towards us. It must have been almost ten-feet wide, when it passed through the lattice.??

"This is ridiculous," I said, watching it approach us. "If they or we are travelling this fast we're moving at hundreds of times the speed of light."

"But," said Elizabeth, with that quizzical expression of hers which usually means a difficult question is coming up. "I know the laws of Relativity forbid it. But why DOES light only travel at a certain speed? I mean, what stops light going faster?"

It's one of those questions where no one listens to what is being asked, like: why do the scales of music start with C instead of A? The usual answer you get is: because it is the middle note of the piano. Missing the point completely.

I fell into the same trap. "In our universe, it's the only speed it can go at."

She raised her eyebrows, telling me I'd better try again.

"Do you mean what constrains it from going faster?" I said, watching the tiny stars pass through us and wondering why I wasn't having a complete panic.

"Yes."

Oh dear.

"No one knows," I said, feeling that during my five years of physics I'd been asking the wrong question. "Its speed has been measured and all motion is constrained by its speed."

"But what would happen if it travelled at twice that speed?"

Both neurons were now required.

"Nothing. I think the world would look the same. As it is constant figure, all the laws of motion and space-time would still work. We would just have a different figure for its speed in our text books."

She thought for a moment then said, "But maybe it does change or can change but because all our measuring sticks change as well we would not know."

Elizabeth is nothing if not tenacious when she has hold of an idea and will not deviate until she has come to a conclusion.

"There is another way of looking at it." I said, "Imagine it as the speed of time."

"You mean the speed we travel along the time dimension in four-dimensional space?"

"You really did absorb all that stuff I gave you on Relativity, didn't you? Have you got any thick cousins I could trade you in for?"

"I would like to help, James, but I am afraid I am regarded as the least intelligent amongst my family, apart from Cousin Henry, of course, but I fear you would find him less accommodating."

I had a brief vision of her moustached cousin in his fox-hunting gear carrying a 12-bore shotgun pointed in my general direction.

More galaxies were appearing and coming towards us. A beautiful orange orb appeared out of my head and drifted through Elizabeth's shoulder.

"They don't seem to be coming from any direction." I said.

"Maybe we are not traveling through space."

"What do you mean?" I said, stalling her while quickly putting my fragile brain back into gear.

"Perhaps we are going backwards or forwards in time."

"Possibly. But why are we so large?"

"In what way?"

"All these stars and galaxies." I said, as half a nebula slowly passed through us. "They're tiny! And… just a minute. If they are real why aren't they burning holes through us?"

"It must be some form of projection for I feel nothing."

"Unless…" At last, a brain wave arrived. "Your point about the speed of light and yardsticks. I think you're right. Someone living in a world with double our speed of light would have double the length of the yard sticks. So, in their world…"

She grabbed me excitedly, "Then everything would seem the same to them as to us but if they could see our world, we would look twice the size. That's why the stars and galaxies are so small. We are in a place where the speed of light must be…Oh… hundreds if not thousands of times faster than in our world. You're a genius, James!"

She hugged me then noticed my puzzled expression and said, "That was what you meant to say. Wasn't it James?"

"Absolutely. Couldn't have put it better myself." I answered truthfully.

E.

For a few moments, we congratulated ourselves on reaching a conclusion on our predicament that had no logical basis or evidence to support it before we remembered that we did not know where we were or what we were supposed to do.

On realisation, our humour left us quickly. James came over to me and pulled me gently to him and we floated slowly, rotating silently, immersing ourselves in stars and galaxies.

"Right. Let's recap our meetings with our little friends the Martians." he said, "They guided us to your home then through one of their telepathic visions they suggested we go back to the cavern."

"Where we found a much-improved version of the Tesla coil." I said.

"Yes, I did notice. And then I pressed the red button. And next thing we find ourselves here. Anything else I've forgotten?"

"My missing sister, perhaps." I said rather pointedly.

"Sorry, too busy thinking about how to get out of here."

I could tell by his apologetic expression that he felt my point and I did not pursue it.

And," he continued looking at his phone, "there's no internet."

Although I love the world of James, its comforts, the advances in medicine, and so forth, I am sometimes overwhelmed by what I would call the deluge of information which bombards our eyes and ears. I have known people who keep the noise of the television and radio on all day. James is not one of those thankfully and in general only switches on a device when there is something of interest to him. However, he does make up for this by the use of his phone. I am quite convinced that this stream of almost random information has a detrimental effect on one's ability to concentrate on one subject long enough to reach a conclusion. The knowledge at our fingertips is not only easily accessible but immense in its variety. To be able at one moment to be able to ascertain the latest in fashion and the next to read a discourse on the latest scientific discovery is a wonder which, in my time, would have necessitated a day of research in the British Library. But I must admit, with a little discipline, these devices do, incredibly, allow knowledge to be acquired at an incredible rate.

Unfortunately, the absence of such facilities in this place made us realise how dependent we had become on these instruments. We were now faced with using as a device for solutions to our problems, our internal computers, which are too heavily influenced by our emotional state affecting their ability for logical deduction. Not helped by the fact that the astral bodies had ceased to move.

J.

Not only had the stars and galaxies stopped moving but those inside the sphere were dissolving or to be more precise, were getting fainter. After a few moments, they had disappeared completely leaving us in an empty cage with just two globes. Then the room started to get darker. I couldn't tell at first what was causing it until I noticed the lattice work was becoming opaque.

Elizabeth came closer. "What is happening?"

Suddenly the room went black. Really black. Only the sound of our breathing and hearts beating told us we still existed.

Out of the darkness a large room or shed began to appear, in the centre of which was an apparatus about twenty-feet-tall, which looked uncannily like a Tesla coil.

A large flash of lightning shot from the apparatus across the room then another. But it wasn't the lightning bolts that concerned me. It was the Victorian gentleman in a dark suit nonchalantly reading a paper, sitting on a chair next to the cylindrical wire cage that surrounded the apparatus.

Chapter Ten

E.

Despite our presence, the gentleman did not seem to notice us and carried on reading his paper, oblivious to the lightning bolts that flew around him. We decided to introduce ourselves for no other reason than we thought having arrived in someone's private apartment unannounced and uninvited it was only polite to do so.

As we approached, rather cautiously I might add in the hope of not being electrocuted, he looked up and folded his paper. Then without a hint of surprise, he said, "Good morning. Sorry, I had forgotten I was receiving visitors. What can I do for you?"

His accent was rather strange, and he had the look of an Eastern European. His head was quite small, and his hair oiled and parted in the centre like so many young men of my time. However, his moustache gave him a rather rakish appearance, though that may have been a trick of the light flashes casting shadows on him.

James surprised me with the politeness and knowledge of his reply. "Good Morning. We are Mr and Mrs Urquhart. Am I speaking to Mr Nikola Tesla?"

"That is correct. What can I do for you?"

"How do you know who he is?" I whispered. But he ignored me and continued.

"We have built and operated an electrical resonant transformer with some success based on a little knowledge of yours."

Mr Tesla's eyes lit up and he interrupted, "You have read my paper?"

"No. I have only read a newspaper cutting but with the aid

of few books on electro-magnetism I managed to put it together."

"Who are you?" said Mr Tesla, now looking a little suspicious of us.

The streams of light continued to play around the room. My head felt a little light and as I touched my hair I heard it crackle.

"It would best to describe us as involuntary time travellers."

A wide smile came upon his face, and he grasped James by both hands.

"You have found a way to time travel using my electro-magnetic apparatus!"

"Not quite. We built the coil, flicked a switch and found ourselves here."

"Where is your machine?"

"I think somewhere in the future, but I can't be sure."

I was pleased he did not answer Mr Tesla's question directly for I did not know what interest he might have in our device.

"And you do not know exactly where it is?"

"Nope." said James, giving what I thought was a blatant lie.

Mr Tesla drew back disappointed. "Then you do not know how you will return."

"'Afraid not. Can you help?"

Mr Tesla's enthusiasm returned. "I will do what I can. Now that I know that time travel is possible."

"Thank you," I said very gratefully, "But pray tell me what year is this?"

"Why, 1895."

"And the date?" said James.

Tesla removed a fob watch from his pocket, "It is nearly midnight. Then it is still the 12th of March."

The bottom nearly fell out of my world because I remembered that the next day Mr Wells said the shift across time occurred and Tesla's laboratory was destroyed.

J.

This was no coincidence. I now realised the Martians had built that Tesla coil at the cavern and designed it so it would transport us to just before the time shift. It was obvious what our mission was. To stop Tesla switching on his apparatus and changing the world. The only thing not obvious was why did they choose us? Oh! And how were we supposed to do it? Suddenly I wondered what time of the day Tesla pressed the red button and I felt that familiar cold sweat on the back of my neck. But that was nothing compared to the realisation that I had just possibly asked him to use his apparatus to help us get back home and doing so would probably cause the shift in time. I tried to think how I could get Elizabeth to understand what I was thinking without annoying Tesla. Luckily my wife has a very intuitive brain.

She said, "Mr Tesla, we are very grateful for your offer. Are you considering using your apparatus to help us?"

"Why, yes. Over the course of the past few months, I have managed to acquire from the Governor of New York the permission to use the electrical power of this whole block. I am convinced this will be sufficient for our needs."

James said, "How much power do you have?"

"Enough to generate between ten million and a hundred million volts in the secondary coil."

I felt a little faint. Elizabeth noticed and steadied my arm.

"OK," I swallowed, "When do we start?"

"As you can see from the lightning discharges it has already begun." he said with the innocent smile of an idiot who doesn't know what he is doing.

And as if to emphasise this a line of plasma which until that moment had been happily playing with the wall, jumped and landed with a thwack on a girder just behind us. Seeing the expression on our faces this had caused he said, "Don't worry you are quite safe where you are."

Neither of us really believed him and in response we instinctively drew closer to each other in the hope that two rather clammy persons huddled together would be a less of a target for the plasma.

Then Elizabeth interjected. "Please excuse me. But if you have already activated your machine before we arrived, what was your purpose?"

And this is why you shouldn't let women in the work place. You hold a meeting with your mates, most of whom are your drinking pals, to solve a problem. Go through rigorous procedures to reach a conclusion and then the token woman comes up with the blindingly obvious by circumventing everything you've said. She's getting a good seeing to when we get home.

Tesla seemed a little embarrassed. "Please humour me but this experiment you see before you is an attempt to communicate with Mars."

"Why?" we both said in unison accompanied by the change of direction of the plasma which had just been passing over us.

That surprised him. I could tell he was obviously used to people regarding him as mentally unstable when he brought the subject up.

"Are you not concerned that I wish to communicate with Mars?"

"No, we communicate with the Martians all the time. Or to be more truthful the little whatsits communicate with us."

"There are people living on Mars?"

"Yes. And on Earth."

His face reminded of me of one those religious paintings of saints who had just seen their first glimpse of heaven. For a moment, my heart felt for him. I knew from what little I had read of his works; he had spent every waking hour of his life for this purpose. He grabbed my hand and shook it.

"Then my experiment will work! All these years, at last through the power of this machine I will contact another race! I knew that by the power of electro-magnetic pulses I would be able to reach across space to other civilisations!"

I swear he danced a little jig at that point.

Unfortunately, I knew what I had to do next and I was feeling a little guilty. For if I couldn't find a way to turn off his machine, we weren't going to get back home. People think scientists are very tenacious in their quests for truth but sadly that's not true. They are very tenacious in trying to prove their theories are correct. There is a difference.

I said to Elizabeth, "I'm going to tell him the truth."

She could see I was having difficulty with it.

"No. Let me tell it, James. He and I are of the same world."

And this is why if there any important decisions to be made about our world, both our sexes should be present.

E.

I could see that Mr Tesla was a man of dedication and therefore to convince him that his life's work would not reach the conclusion he wished would require some work. I have come to realise this is often difficult for men for they are trained from birth to demonstrate that they are successful in the eyes of others. We women do not help, for money generally resides with successful men and for a woman to raise a family with hope of aspirations, a man with money, especially in the world in which I was raised, is required.

Success is relative, of course. James is not rich by any means and often we must count our pennies but we have a home together and health. And of course, love brings much comfort. I do sometimes wonder if I had stayed in my own world how much the need for money would have had to compete with that emotion.

I also wonder why I digress so often from the subject in question.

"Mr Tesla." I began, "You may not enjoy what I have to say but please remember that my husband tells me that your work will become so famous that they will name the unit of... oh, what was it, James?"

"Magnetic field strength. One tesla is a weber per square metre in SI units."

"Yes, sorry. I can assure you, Mr Tesla, that whenever that is measured it will be measured in units of tesla."

I think he visibly melted with pride.

"But I must tell you that if you leave that machine on you will alter the fabric of time and space and transport the world's population to a new world."

To my surprise this did not cause him consternation.

"Will it be a better place?"

"Different." said James.

"I see. Then what will happen if I turn off on my apparatus?"

"None of this will happen. Elizabeth and I will have a nice picnic. Wells won't turn up and spoil it. And we won't build a Tesla coil to come back to tell you not to turn yours on."

"I see," said Mr Tesla. He thought for a few moments, turning to his machine and back to us several times. Then his expression changed to an almost sardonic smile and he said, "Much as I would not like to ruin your picnic, the problem is my apparatus cannot be turned off."

"What do you mean? Just turn the power supply off."

"That will have no effect." Another bolt of lightning hit the cage, "I have designed it so that it is self-perpetuating."

"That's impossible." said James, "The first law of thermodynamics won't allow it."

"Impossible? Why don't you turn it off? The circuit breaker is there." he said pointing to two very thick cables which terminated in the kind of circuit breaker you only find on large power stations.

And as if to prove his point another large bolt of lightning shot across the room.

"OK. I'll do it," said James. And he walked over to the apparatus.

"James! What are you doing?" I shouted and caught his arm.

"I'm going to do what I came here to do!" And he snatched his arm away.

Then he walked over and with only a moment's hesitation and one last look at me he pulled down the bar.

Nothing happened.

Bolts of lightning continued to bounce around the room.

Mr Tesla was smiling, "See. It now powers itself. The electricity was required only to start the process. Now you see what I have achieved? This is what I will give to the world. An inexhaustible supply of free electricity!"

"I don't care," said James, now very angry, possibly because his 'heroic' action had been to no avail. Then he lost his temper, picked up Mr Tesla's wooden chair and threw it at the large cage surrounding the apparatus.

The last thing I remember was a blinding flash of blue light.

J.

I'm not quite sure why I threw that chair. Though when asked I always say it was the only way to short circuit the Tesla coil and NOT, as someone not far from me suggested, the result of a fit of temper.

We awoke to find ourselves back in that dark place again with the stars and galaxies drifting through the lattice. By their light, I could see Elizabeth in a kind of suspended animation. I drifted over and awoke her.

She looked around. "Are we still here, James? I had a dream that we had met Mr Tesla and you had destroyed his machine and saved the world."

"It must have been a dream if you found me doing heroic things."

She pulled herself to me and closing her eyes she whispered, "I am so tired. Wake me when we are back home."

The stars and galaxies continued to pass through us. Their slow majestic movement became, for some reason, quite soporific and I joined her in sleep.

Chapter Eleven

J.

I drifted in an and out of a fitful slumber. In the darkness images of Mr Tesla's laboratory flashed before me. The two globes of Mars and Earth began to glow, slowly getting brighter. As my eyes adjusted to the new light I began to see the room again. It had changed. The lattice had disappeared to be replaced by rough-hewn stone. It looked familiar. I nudged Elizabeth awake. She raised her head from my shoulder.

"James! We are back in the time cavern!"

As recognisable features came into view, I said, "I'm not convinced we ever left."

"What do you mean?"

"I think when I pressed that button we were jettisoned temporarily out of our time and space."

"To where? To when?"

"Neither. I think the shock was so intense it caused a hole to appear in the fabric of space-time."

She thought for a moment then said, "I can understand what you say, for in my mind I can see a hole in space, but space is empty. How can you have a hole in it? Unless... Oh I remember. I read that it could be filled with, what did they call them?"

"Virtual particles. Pairs of matter and anti-matter particles. And stop reading my physics books. I'll be out of a job if the college finds out how much you know."

"You shouldn't have bought me that computer and introduced me to all those lectures. Now, where was I? Ah yes. So, are you saying that the discharge of electricity blew these particles out of a region of space?"

119

"Quite possible." I said, "And that lattice we saw around us was perhaps the boundary of that hole."

I tried to think how much energy would be needed to create a hole the size of the cavern and gave up. The maths was beyond me. The Martians, who I suspected had built the Tesla coil, live in a four or perhaps five-dimensional world. They are thus able to exist a little in the future and the past as well as the present. This means they see us in a different way. I have written this before but it needs repeating. Imagine a film of yourself recorded on one of those old reel cameras. Then cut up each frame and place each frame on top of each other and glue them together so you have a stack or block of frames. If you carefully cut out of the block your image you will have an impression of how a Martian sees us. We would seem to be a blur stretching into the past and future. Now imagine if you could tap into the energy from the future and past. God knows what forces of nature they can control.

Elizabeth was also thinking about it. "Do you think that within this hole the speed of light was not contained?"

A word of warning to any scientist who while time-travelling picks up and marries an intelligent Victorian girl. If you keep reminding her that your scientific knowledge is far more advanced than hers she will quickly remind you how many black holes there are in your philosophy. I have seriously considered bringing her along to one of my lectures at college where I think she could give an excellent discourse on the 'Unified Theory and Castles Built on Sand'. AND destroy one or two of the cockier students who are a constant thorn in my side in the process. But back to her question.

"I think the question of speed is irrelevant. In such a hole, nothing would exist. The way those stars and galaxies moved it implied we did not exist either."

"But we were real. Weren't we?"

"Were we? Perhaps we were just caught in a vision created by the Martians."

"Oh, I see. I think...." She stopped and quickly looked around the room. "But where are Flory and the Wells?"

"Perhaps they've legged it."

She grabbed my arm. "Or maybe they were destroyed or transported to another time or place!"

"Let's go with my idea first."

In the dim light, we scanned the room. Strange ghostly shapes began to appear by the walls which slowly took shape.

"It's the time control consoles!" I shouted. "What's going on?"

And then the Martian Tesla Coil began to appear.

"I don't like this." I said pointing at the coil which was almost solid now. "If this thing starts up again God knows what will happen to us this time."

"I agree. We need to leave."

"Ok. Two options. First, play with those two globes and see where they take us or second, leave by that door."

"I think we need to know when we are first, James. Luckily, we are in Victorian clothing so modesty will not be an issue."

I looked for the date and time dials, but they weren't there.

I said, "You're right. We need a reference point. I don't think we humans like being out of time. We always need to know when we are."

"I cannot but agree. Even though we move through time there is always some comfort when we find WHEN we are."

"So that's decided. We go outside and have a look. The only problem is," scanning the room, "where's the damn door?"

There was no sign of it.

"It must be over there." She said, pointing at where I thought we'd come in.

"Maybe it hasn't materialised yet. Let's try feeling the wall and see if we can find it."

A loud thwack sound came from behind us. Then another.

"Jeeze! That machine's starting up again!" I said.

We frantically felt along the wall. There was another loud spark and this time the room flashed white.

Real panic was gripping me now. Then Elizabeth shouted, "I have found it! It's here. Look!"

Her hand and arm had disappeared through the wall.

"Come on, James! Hurry!" And as another lightning spark lit the room she vanished.

Chapter Twelve

E.

I found myself in pitch black once more. What had I done? Was I in the tunnel? I carefully put my hands out. Fear washed over me as I wondered what I might meet. Then, thankfully, I felt a damp stone wall. I moved slowly along it but panicked when I realised I did not know which way I was going. Cold perspiration ran down my face. I could not think any more. And where was James? There is something about absolute darkness. It presses on you like an invisible force. I could feel my eyes frantically moving in the hope of catching a glimmer of light but finding none.

After a while when my senses had returned or possibly left me completely, I do not know which, I decided to move back about three feet to where I thought I started and find the door by which I entered. Again, I tentatively put out my hands then, I swear I nearly died of fright because something warm and clammy brushed my hand and grasped it!

A strangled voice yelled out, "Oh my God! What the...... Oh! It's you, Elizabeth! Thank God! I thought I'd found a Martian or something worse! Come here."

I felt two arms envelop me and pull me roughly to him. His hot breath caressed my ear: "Are you ok?" then before I could reply he whispered, "Mmh! You smell nice and sweaty."

How he manages to turn things into an intimate compliment, I do not know.

"James! Only horses sweat..." I protested.

"Yeah, I know. Ladies glow. Well, you're glowing quite a bit."

His comment did not deter me from clinging on to him. I

replied, "And so are you. I nearly died when you touched me."

"Me too."

We held each other, until our breathing and heart beats had calmed enough to think. The blackness was becoming oppressive again.

"Which way do you think we should go?" I said.

"I'm not going back in there. Trouble is we've left everything behind."

Despair. Then I remembered.

"Not everything, James. I still have my handbag."

"How've you still got that?"

"A lady always carries a handbag."

"You know what I mean."

"I do. I believe we are still wearing our clothes because they are part of us, unless due to some further mystery you are regarding me as nature intended."

I felt his hands move over my body. I should have expected that response.

"You seem to be dressed." he said as I tried vainly to follow in the dark where his hands were wandering.

"Are you acquainted with a person called the Octopus?" I said.

"Nope, why?"

"Oh. Nothing. Now stop it! Anyway, you know how you often joke about ladies and their handbags?"

"Yes, and I do know there are things I realise a girl needs to carry with her at all times."

"But apart from those, a handbag is also useful for carrying other items which a gentleman might wonder why they were needed."

"Like the contents of my garage, I suppose?"

"Nothing like your garage."

Despite the dark I managed to open my reticule and

rummage inside. "Oh! It is somewhere in here. Why is it the object you need is always at the bottom? Do not answer that either, James."

I eventually found what I was looking for. "Ah! Here it is."

"What?"

I did not mean to nearly blind him with the torch light nor cause him to bang his head on the wall.

I examined his head to ensure his brain was no more damaged than usual, and after a few moments he recovered. Though not without a rather rude admonishment of my action which I will not record.

By the aid of the torch we proceeded down the tunnel away from the cavern in the hope of finding a sanctuary. Eventually we arrived at the wooden vestry door. James said, "Shall we open it or shall we carry on?"

"Open it." I said. "At least this is familiar. But first see if you can look through that keyhole to see what or who might be there. I confess I have still not recovered from that time we 'borrowed' those parishioners' coats. For all we know we have been transported back to that time and they are waiting for us."

He peered through the latch hole. "Can't tell. It's dark. I'll have to open it."

Before I could stop him, he lifted the latch and pushed the door. It moved without a sound. We waited. Hearing nothing, I shone the torch. To my relief, I found it was the familiar vestry complete with altar and candles.

We carefully entered on tiptoe, together this time and holding hands.

"Well, this could be any time. We'll have to go into the nave and hope we aren't too out of place."

J.

The nave was full of tourists wearing the normal casual garb of the early 21st century and on the pillars were large screens displaying the services of the day.

"We're back home!" I said.

"Oh, what a relief. But is it our world?"

"Only one way to find out."

We both almost ran to the nave exit and out on to the street. The familiar traffic of cars and lorries passed down the road.

"Looks OK." I said.

Just as I was going to decide what to do next, a family who were standing near the entrance with two children came up to us.

The bloke, whom I presumed was the father, said, "Are you the guides for the Ghost Tour?"

"Nope." I said, not really paying attention.

"So, what you dressed in that gear for?"

"We have just come back from 1895." I said half-jokingly to impress the children.

"Cor! You doing time travellers like Dr Who?" said the oldest child.

"No, we're not," I replied.

"Where's your Tardis?" chipped in the youngest.

"What is a Tardis, James?" said Elizabeth.

"It's a fictional…."

"What?" said the youngest, interrupting and turning to Elizabeth, "You don't know what the Tardis is? Everyone know the Tardis."

"Well, I can assure you, I do not." said Elizabeth, giving me a blank look.

"Corr! Listen to her la-di-da accent," said the oldest to his dad.

"Shhh!" said the father, "They're acting, son. She's

pretending she's a posh Victorian."

Elizabeth looked at the father, then at me, then down at the child and said to it rather haughtily, "For your information I am, as you people refer to us, a Victorian. And I should remind you, it is not good manners to refer to a person who is present in the third person."

The child looked around a bit bewildered then said, "Where's the other one then?"

"Whom do you mean?" she said, looking around as well.

"The other one. This third person."

"Did you not learn grammar at school?" she said.

And then it kicked off.

"Oi! Who are you to tell my son how to talk?" joined in the mother.

"How dare you speak to me like that!" said Elizabeth and turned to me with that expression indicating it was time to show how I defended her honour.

Luckily the dad got in first, "Hold on! It's a play, Doreen. They're doing characters."

During this discussion, I noticed several other people had gathered around us in a circle. At this point one came over to me and put a pound in my cap which I was still holding in my hand while in the church, and said, winking at me, "You want to put a few coins in that hat first so it looks like you're doing well."

Before I could reply the youngest child said, "Ask them where's his time machine, Dad."

"We don't have one." I said.

"What? How can you do your show without a time machine?"

"We're not doing a show." I repeated.

"What you dressed like that for?" said the father.

I thought quickly on my feet but not as quickly as Elizabeth.

"We are going to a fancy-dress party, if you must know." She said looking rather crossly in my general direction.

"Ooh! 'if we must know'," imitated the youngest. I was beginning to wonder whether the laws on corporal punishment needed an exception for small brats.

I could see by Elizabeth's expression that she concurred but unfortunately, she did not keep her thoughts to herself.

"I think, child," she said bending down so she was only about a foot from its face, "you need a box on the ears from your mother to help learn some manners."

"Who do you think you are, telling us to hit Billy?" said the father.

"She's my wife." I interceded, eyeing him at the same time and reaching the conclusion he looked like he worked out at the gym every day.

"Your wife?" he said, looking a bit incredulous.

"Yeah. She's from a different world."

"Really? I can believe it. Looks like you've got a handful there."

I decided not to answer that question. Though unfortunately I think Elizabeth noticed that I involuntarily nodded in agreement.

And so, the conversation continued in the predictable downward spiral, interrupted by occasional cheers from the gathering audience who obviously thought this was all part of the 'act' until Elizabeth took my arm and said., "I am not staying here to be insulted any more, James! Take me away from here to somewhere where people have manners and treat a lady with respect."

"Ooh! She thinks she's a lady," said the oldest child to everyone in the now quite considerable crowd who burst into laughter and applause.

We took our cue and left rather red-faced and walked

quickly into town without looking back. On the way, I am sure we were asked at least a dozen times if we were doing the Ghost Tour. By the time we reached the town centre the language of my replies to this question, to use Elizabeth's vernacular, was in need of some considerable moderation.

E.

It must have been the stress of the Tesla Coil which caused me to react the way I did with that child. Though even James admitted he was near to the point of beating it himself. I can normally cope with the manners of James' world though I confess I often confuse direct questions and banter with rudeness, but I have learnt to hold my tongue until I have ascertained the direction and temper of the conversation. I wonder if or when we have children whether I will be able to balance kindness with sufficient discipline. I would hate to be referred to in my old age as the terrible old crone whom children should avoid.

We decided   that we needed to find a route back to our cottage as quickly as possible. Not least because, just before we reached Midhurst's town centre we were met, or should I say accosted, by four persons dressed in an assortment of Victorian clothes who wished to know why we were impersonating their ghost tour. When we denied this accusation, one of them pointed at James' cap and demanded to know where all that money had come from. We both immediately looked and noticed to our surprise and embarrassment we had accumulated over £10! Up to that point I must admit I thought I had had enough arguments for one day. However, during the altercation that ensued, I was quite surprised how much venom James and I still had stored in reserve.

Eventually a truce was reached when they accepted that we were going to a fancy-dress party and more importantly when we agreed to offer our hard-earned monies to their charity. Unfortunately, just as we were about to take their leave, to our amazement Flory appeared.

"Oh, Lizzy, it is you! I thought you were all ghosts from our time."

"If I hear the word ghost one more time..." said James.

"I thought you were lost, Flory!" I exclaimed, ignoring his remark and embracing her warmly, "How did you get here? And where are Mr and Mrs Wells?"

"After the flash, we ran into the tunnel and by aid of Mr Wells' matches we arrived at the vestry. However, when I entered and turned to wait for them, they had disappeared!"

"Not surprising," said James, "he only lives in 1895."

"So pray tell me what year are we in, Lizzy? It looks like James' world."

"We think it's 2015. Is that right?" said James, turning to the party with us.

It was then we noticed the four people next to us were staring at us with their mouths open.

The older gentleman came to his senses first. "I do not quite follow your conversation, but I take it this lady," pointing at Flory, "is going to your fancy-dress party as well."

My sister takes some pride in arranging her appearance and of consequence is often late for engagements and soirees. His comment, therefore, was not well received.

"Fancy dress? How dare you be so impertinent! This outfit, I assure you, is the latest in travel fashion and unlike your apparel, was not obtained from a charity jumble!"

Rather than respond in like fashion they regarded each other with some amusement followed by some whispering which I was convinced was at our expense. The gentleman then apologised for causing us any offence and wished us a pleasant day. The reason for this change of heart did not become apparent until later when James told me that he had overheard part of their conversation and on the promise that I would not become angry with him said that they had come to the conclusion that my sister and I were out on licence from a sanatorium and as a consequence we should be treated with kid gloves.

And to think I was only worried about my modesty when I arrived here!

As we watched the group walk off James reminded me that we had still not ascertained when we were.

Let's get a paper," he said, "And then I'll try and draw some money from the bank. That should be a good test of what timeline we are in."

We crossed the road to a newsagent and bought a local paper.

The date on the local newspaper was the 24th of March, 2015, the same day we had arrived at Stedham for our picnic.

Chapter Thirteen

J.

We were back where we started. But for some reason I didn't feel we'd done what the Martians and Wells wanted us to do. But first I wanted to get back into the outside my world and find. And that meant getting my car back.

I said, "If the date's right on that paper, that means my car should still be at Stedham. Let's go and pick it up and go back home and change our clothes. Are you alright with that, Flory?"

"Yes please. I will be glad not to be an object of attention."

Elizabeth said, "But how shall we get to it? It must be three miles from here at least. Shall we take a bus?"

"No point. In my world country buses only run if there is an 'r' in the month and it's a Tuesday. We'll have to take a taxi."

The taxi driver was quite friendly and actually believed our story about the fancy-dress party which was quite a relief to all of us. Thankfully my car was still there by the gate and we all piled in.

"So," I said, "now that some semblance of normality has returned, home we go. But first I'm going to phone my sister to meet us there."

The journey was uneventful which after the last few days was quite a surprise to us all. The sun was shining. The countryside looked like normal Sussex. In fact, by the time we arrived back in Chichester we were all quite relaxed and feeling that the adventure was behind us by some distance.

I parked the car. Jill was already standing at the door.

"Hello, you lot. Oh hi, Flory, lovely outfit. Come and have some tea and tell me what've you all been caught up in this time?"

E.

There is nothing like a full meal after an adventure to relax the mind. This feeling was much aided by Jill, whom I love very much, being her normal self.

"So, Jim. I understand you saved the world by losing your rag and throwing a chair at Mr Tesla."

"I did NOT lose it! And I threw it at the apparatus. Isn't that right, Elizabeth?"

There are times when a wife must be dutiful and support her husband. I must endeavour to find one such time but for now...

"You did give the impression," I said, gently putting my hand on his knee, "that you were a little miffed and were looking in the general direction of Mr Tesla when you threw it."

"It was a calculated scientific gamble! I thought the chair being metal I might somehow short, or earth, the machine."

"And I understand you gave up the chance for the world to have free electricity just so you could get back home with my sister." said Flory, having a dig as well. "Such gallantry and devotion. They will write stories and poems about it."

"And in return when I need support from my dutiful wife in supporting my story," he said, waving a finger at me, quite humorously I was glad to see, "she shops me!"

Seeing that the only response was laughter, he said, "OK. You're right. I admit I lost it. But it worked though, didn't it? We're all back safely home. And that's all I care about."

Noticing poor James had become rather red in the face, Jill quickly changed the subject.

"So, where do you think your lovebirds Mr and Mr Wells

are now? Do you think they're shacked up together somewhere and making up for twenty years of abstinence?"

"The last time I saw them," said Flory, doing very well with only a slight blush whilst ignoring the second question, "was by the vestry door in the tunnel."

"Perhaps they went on to the Coaching Inn or the Angel." I said.

"Or back into the cavern." said James.

"I don't think so," said Flory, "They were as scared as I was. We ran like the wind down that tunnel."

"Then let's assume they went to the Inn. Do you think they then went back to Isabel's house?" I said.

"Wouldn't be my choice, if I was Isabel." said Jill, "I'd be worried about the other Wells turning up. Can you imagine? There's your husband waiting for you and you turn up with his doppelganger. Boom! Bad enough when you're with one boyfriend and you bump into another one that you're seeing. Same with your girlfriends, isn't it, James?"

"Couldn't possibly comment." James replied, with an enigmatic smile that left me wondering whether I had been part of one of those ménages de trois. But before I could comment he rather unfairly goaded my sister, who had only recently turned twenty, with the same question.

"You haven't got two on the go at the moment, have you, Flory?"

"I could not comment either, James, as I have lost count of the number of suitors who are currently competing for my affections."

"Excellent, Flory. You tell him," laughed Jill and we all joined in.

Sensing the mood could be exploited further, I said, "Would you like to see James in the knickerbockers that Flory obtained for him?"

"Oh, yes please!" they both said.

"Well you can't. I got rid of them." he said hotly.

"Give me your phone, James," I said.

"Why?" he said removing it from his pocket, "Oh No! Don't tell me you took a photo!"

I snatched it from him and threw it to Jill. "Here you are, Jill. I think you will find it easier to find them than me."

Jill took the phone before poor James could get to it and quickly found the photographs. "Oh yes! That's going on TwitFace." And then touched her phone to his. "Got it! And... off it goes to the great party in the sky. Ooh! I've got five likes already and one... two....three comments! Would you like to hear them, Jim?"

"NO!" said James, covering his face with his hands.

"One's from Jane. Remember her?"

"Who?" he said.

"You know. My school friend you forgot to give a lift home to, from that party."

I am not quite sure what sound he made but a vision of a cornered fox who knew it was about to meet its end came to mind.

Eventually he recovered and stood up. "OK, you've had your fun now," he said, retrieving his phone from his sister. "I'm going to get changed. This linen is chafing in all the wrong places. And I suggest you two do as well otherwise I'll have to uprate the air conditioning in my car to stop it smelling like my old granny."

"Then you should have thought twice before courting and marrying a girl who was as old as your grandmother." I replied, enjoying the exchange.

Then Jill devilishly changed sides. "I'm sure you told me, Jim, when you first became besotted with Elizabeth," (his face was a picture) "that you liked the smell of mothballs and girls who only washed once a month."

There then followed a rather violent but humorous cushion fight between pairs of siblings after which it was all agreed a change of clothing was necessary.

J.
Outnumbered and outgunned again!

Chapter Fourteen

E.

I arose quite late in the morning and doused myself blissfully in the canopy shower for what felt like half an hour.

I then sprinkled my nineteenth century clothes with an eau-de-toilette and after convincing myself that they did not smell of mothballs, packed them into a portmanteau.

Jill was kind enough to allow us to borrow some of her modern clothes as I thought, after the exertions of our adventures, mine required a long visit to a laundry.

After choosing items which were a reasonable compromise between modesty and the hot Spring weather, we all sat down to enjoy a late breakfast, or as James called it, 'a full-metal heart-stopping brunch' peppered by a grilling of Flory and her social life. Her main complaint was Father whom she thought kept her on too tight a rein and quizzed her intently on any beau that might come up in conversation.

"It is an annoyance," she said, "and when he is away on business, he packs me off to Aunt Harriet in Chichester!"

"Aunt Harriet!" I exclaimed. Uncle Charlie, her late husband, when he was alive, was a child's best friend. At the drop of a hat he would whisk you off to a fair or circus and treat you to as much ice cream and sweets as you could manage. Aunt Harriet, on the other hand, thought the best place for a young child was a darkened drawing room with a selection of books on manners, etiquette and the best way to get to heaven. I had long concluded I was going to the other place when I died but I used to console myself with the belief that at least I would see Uncle Charlie again.

"The problem is," said Jill, "What are we going to do with you, Flory? You are very welcome to stay in this time if

Elizabeth is happy with that. Though you may find that you won't be able to depend on me completely for chaperone duties."

"I've got some friends who I'm sure can help out in that area," said James.

"Actually, Jim, from my experience, I think it's YOUR friends who could do with a bit of chaperoning," said Jill.

"What - including Sean?"

Sean was Jill's long standing beau with whom she lived in Chichester. He is a gentle soul who looked after her very well. His only problem is that when he and James get together they adopt the manners of uncontrollable children.

Flory thankfully interrupted before Jill could reply. "I thank you all very much. It is a very attractive proposition but... but I have someone waiting for me."

I just managed to squeeze Jill's leg hard enough under the table to arrest the enquiry I knew was coming.

J.

As I sat back, loosening my belt a little after the extra two sausages, I said, "So, where could our happy couple, the Wells, have gone and even more importantly when are they?"

"If Jill's suggestion is correct," said Elizabeth, "they could be anywhere. He is, I believe quite famous and could have many friends."

"But Flory thought they carried on down the tunnel which suggests they are stuck in this world with all their friends dead." said Jill, "He'll have no modern money and he'll be wandering around in that blue cap and blazer."

"Then I hope he doesn't meet the Ghost Tour people," Elizabeth said, "Imagine how the conversation would go."

"Yeah, or those wonderful children we met." I said.

"Anyway, do we care what's happened to him? We might have got rid of him at last."

"He knows where we live, James."

"God! You're right. I'm not going to spend the rest of my life wondering who's knocking on our door. So, where is he?" I said.

"Why don't you see what happened to him in this world?" suggested Elizabeth.

"Good point. Let's have a look," and I got out my phone and looked him up.

"God, there's loads on him. Ah! Here he is. Just check around 1895."

"Is he here in this world?" said Jill.

"Yep. And he's run off with ...... and divorced Isabel!"

"But he claimed he'd never married her!" said Elizabeth.

"Our Wells didn't. So, the one who disappeared in the church must have been the one that did."

"And I bet he was the one who was off to have a bit of clandestine fun with his floozy." Said Jill.

"And then just by amazing coincidence, we arrive with our Wells." I said.

"James!" said Elizabeth. "I've just remembered. He made us wait outside the church until the clock struck two before we went in. Did he know his doppelganger was still in there and was waiting for him to disappear?"

"Devious little beggar, isn't he?" said Jill.

"I'm not sure he knew. He was quite surprised to see Isabel."

"True." Said Elizabeth, "And he was not exactly forth coming in affection when he realised who she was."

I was just about to put the phone back in my pocket when I thought I'd look up Isabel Wells.

"Just checked our Isabel in this world. She married again in

1902 to some Yorkshire man called Edward Fowler Saville Smith."

"Sounds a bit posh. What did he do?"

"Printer. Let's see what he left in probate. Oh. Only £150. And ... just a minute. He says he left it to his Widow Margaret Ann Smith!"

"Isabel must have died or they divorced and he married again. When did she die?"

"Mm, 1931. Left him £1300. Not bad."

"So! Where does that get us?"

"It suggests our Mr Wells is the one with Isabel. But if so, where could he have gone? As Jill said, he would not last long in this world."

The obvious answer came to me immediately. "Damn! Of course! Your home!"

"What do you mean?"

"Remember who your grandfather bought it from?"

"Yes! Mr Wells himself."

"And perhaps that's where we will find him."

'There's only one way to find out."

"And we might find a way to get Flory home."

E.

The discovery of the true story of my father, grandfather, Mr Wells and our home is still a shock.

I still do not understand the importance of our home in the cause of the temporal shifts. We have discovered that it exists in many alternate time lines and is an ancient and special place that may have contained a portal to Mars.

In at least one world it remains in a time stasis in 1895. It is beyond reason. And all that time that I had been travelling in time with James my incorrigible father knew what was happening!

But I must return to our visit.

We all left together in James' carriage dressed in modern clothes though we took the precaution of packing and bringing garments of my period. My occupation in James' world as a lecturer on the fashions of the late nineteenth century has given me an advantage, for I have accumulated a considerable amount of clothing from the period. James regarded our box room as my equivalent of his garage and at times, when I have spent half a morning rummaging for something I needed, only to remember I had given or lent it to an acquaintance, I can only agree.

As we approached Hamgreen I was glad to see that the dark fir forest had been replaced with the natural beech woodland of Sussex again. At last we came to the old stone pillars of the Lodge and slowly entered the gravel drive. We were now all rather pensive in anticipation of what we would find. I did not notice a time shift but when we arrived in the courtyard I could see by the wooden sash windows of the vine-covered, ashlar facade that we had returned to the nineteenth century.

James alighted from the carriage first and walked across to the front door and pulled the bell. We waited but there was no answer. He tried again then gave the door quite a shove, with no avail. Still no answer. He came back and peering through the window of the carriage where we all sat said. "Looks like no one is in. That's the only thing I wasn't expecting."

I suggested we try the tradesmen's entrance.

We opened the side gate and walked into the kitchen garden. It was well tended with rows of onions, potatoes, and cabbages.

"Someone's looking after it," said Jill. Before I could reply the door opened and there was our father dressed in black coat and tails.

"Hello," he said, "I did not recognise you at first in your modern dress."

Both Flory and I instantly, from habit and without success, tried to pull down the hem of our skirts to below our knees. He noticed and with a smile said, "We have company in the parlour, therefore I suggest you change into something more, how shall I say, suitable. You may take the back stairs of the kitchen."

As we made our way through the kitchen, Jill whispered to me, "What's wrong with your men? I bet they spend all their lives trying to look up girls' skirts. Then when you show off your legs they tell you to cover them up."

I surprised myself by replying, "You know the answer. Less seen, more want."

She stifled a laugh with her hand, "Elizabeth! I'm shocked. What a suggestion."

From the hallway, we could hear several voices in the parlour.

"Sounds like a party," said Jill. "Do you think I'll get to chat up some real live Victorian men?"

"What about Sean?" I said.

"It's only for research. Come on. Can't miss out on an opportunity like this. What year is it?"

"1895, I think."

"Damn! Aren't those ridiculous mutton chops back in?"

"Yes' And twice the size. It is like wearing balloons on one's arms."

"Helps fend off the gropers though. What about evening wear? Plenty of cleavage?"

"Yes. You can rely on our men folk not to let that go out of fashion."

"Oh well." said Jill, taking my arm, "Let's get changed, then best breast forward."

J.

Once again, I was treated to wearing one of her father's suits. I managed to get it all on except the white starched bib, or whatever you call it, which kept on curling up at the bottom. The bow tie, as usual, was beyond me. I eventually managed to wrap it around the winged collar in what my dearest refers to, with much hilarity, as the Urquhart Knot.

I must make a mental note to carry one of those clip-on ties.

From what I could remember, ladies were not allowed to enter a room with mixed company without a male escort. This required the chosen gentleman to wait, patiently, outside the lady's dressing room until she emerged and then escort her to the soiree. Apparently, banging on the door and shouting, "How long are you going to be? You've been in there over an hour!" is regarded as bad manners.

There is a further complication if there are several ladies and only one dressing room. This means you can find yourself with half a dozen other gentlemen who, every time the door opens, all attempt to claim the lady emerging as theirs. As sometimes the ladies will look completely different from when they went in, a romantic evening can often end very quickly.

I have suggested to Elizabeth that perhaps the ladies could all come out together, but she said that would be less fun especially as it is customary to spy through the keyhole to see who's waiting then draw lots to decide who goes first.

Ah! Girls and romance, eh?

On this occasion, Flory had gone to her own room and Jill was sharing Elizabeth's. Once dressed I went across the landing to Elizabeth's bedroom and waited. Eventually after

Hell had frozen over, melted again and refroze, they both came out together.

Somehow, they had managed to pile their hair up into complicated buns but also let it fall in waves to their necks. Really impressive. Elizabeth had a green embroidered silk dress nicely cut away at the front to reveal just enough. Jill's was a yellow-orange and managed to make sure her cleavage was a distraction. They both had ridiculous mutton chop sleeves and long white gloves.

I really don't understand how girls transform themselves into beautiful objects of attraction. All I have to do is put on a pair of trousers, shirt and jacket and brush my hair and I'm ready. I can only presume that when we blokes aren't around they spend their whole-time practising dressing and undressing, doing their hair and trying on makeup. I've no idea how they find time to become intelligent and full of knowledge as well.

"What are you doing here, Jim? said Jill, "Were you spying through the keyhole?"

"No! Apparently, ladies can't be seen without an escort. Isn't that right, Elizabeth?"

"That is right. And today you have the honour of escorting and protecting two beautiful and demure young ladies to the drawing room," she said. They then put on their sweetest beguiling and innocent smiles and performed an exaggerated curtsey for me.

"I think it's me who needs protecting." I said.

"Don't worry, James. We will look after you," said Elizabeth coming up close to my cheek and allowing a wondrous perfume fragrance to envelop me. "But not before I have rearranged the Urquhart knot into some semblance of a tie and given you a monocle."

"A what?" I said as she produced an eye glass attached to a

145

leather string.

"It is all the rage for the young set. Put it in your eye."

After about a minute of squinting I managed to hold it there.

"It's just plain glass!" I said.

"It is fashion, James. It is not an aid for observation."

Then each put an arm through mine and escorted me downstairs.

After a small discussion in the hallway to decide who should go in first we entered the drawing room together and were confronted by a mixed bunch of about a dozen people, in the centre of which stood Mr and Mrs Wells. Though which Mr Wells it was I had yet to discover.

When they saw us, they all turned and stopped talking which caused me to mentally go up and down my clothes in the hope I hadn't left any behind or undone. Then Elizabeth's father came over to us and after giving me a quick inspection like a regimental sergeant major and complimenting me on my tie, introduced us to the audience.

It seems Mr and Mrs Wells had got married and Elizabeth's father had thrown a small party for them and their friends. I recognised Mr Hyatt, the school teacher. His wife, who was dressed in what looked like a church-grey crinoline gave a polite smile and small curtsey. What I wasn't expecting was Henry, Elizabeth's cousin, who looked the same age as when we had left him in the 1870s. He greeted us very pleasantly. "Good to see you, Urquhart. I must say this place looks a little off colour since my last visit and as for the ladies' costumes well - the sleeves are a little outlandish."

"Yes. This place always surprises me. Do you mind telling me what year this is?"

"Why it is 1875, Mr Urquhart. Are you unwell?"

"Not more than normal. So, what brings you here?"

"Had a sudden invite from Flory yesterday. Couple of friends had arrived for a weekend shoot. Flory was kind enough to invite them as well."

At that moment, Flory joined us and slipped her arm through Henry's. This action was noted by my entourage immediately who both pinched my arms to signal that I was not to comment on pain of death, or worse.

Beside him were two men, whom I presumed were his two toff friends from the Bollinger Club, each wearing a monocle. I was having difficulty keeping mine in place and talking at the same time. Eventually, Elizabeth took pity on me and removed it as she said I had acquired the expression of someone who had been poked in the eye.

At that point a butler who looked extraordinarily like Smethers and confirmed this by winking at me offered us large glasses of a green aperitif.

It was delicious and had the immediate effect of relaxing me. I later learnt it was absinthe and even later, I wished I hadn't drunk four glasses of it.

Smethers and I got on quite well, as I think I did with all the servants. Mainly because they thought I was one of them. I'd like to think that was probably true and also because I really felt the oppression of the working class was a genuine problem in Elizabeth's time. Elizabeth gets quite defensive when I mention this and reminds me there was no social net for the poor in her time.

The first of Henry's friends to whom we were introduced, whose name I have forgotten, was a member of Henry's hunt and his cricket team. I didn't discover whether he had a job or even whether he knew what one was. He had greasy ginger hair parted down the middle, a matching moustache and smelt of stale tobacco.

Unable to get a rapport with me on my sporting prowess,

he asked, "Have you just come down?"

"Yes," I said.

"And where were you, Sir?"

"In my wife's bedroom." I replied, knowing he meant had I just finished University. He pretended not to notice my excellent riposte and turned his attention to Jill. Oh dear!

"And may I ask if this charming lady is your wife?"

"No, she's not. She's my sister, Jillian Urquhart. This is my wife...."

But he ignored me and Elizabeth and concentrated on Jill who was still portraying her sweet innocent look and said, "I am pleased to meet your acquaintance."

"Thank you, sir." She said and curtsied.

Then with what I presumed was his one and only chat up line he said to her, "Have you come out?"

"No, sir. Though I have thought about it. But I have concluded that despite men's foibles and their one-track minds regarding women, I do prefer their company for the pleasure of satisfying my requirements."

His monocle fell into his drink, splashing green liquor on to his white bib. She then curtsied again with a smile and moved on to the next 'hooray henry'.

"I think he was asking if you had just come out into society," I whispered.

"Yes, I know. Fun, isn't it?" she giggled, taking another swig of her absinthe.

The next one was a little older and had managed to grow a pair of side whiskers. He had the look, like Henry, of a military man who didn't mind standing in a long red line catching cannonballs. I noticed he immediately recognised Elizabeth.

I introduced myself to which he replied, "Ah! Mr Urquhart. I am pleased to meet with your acquaintance. Edward Ponsonby, late of the 35th Sussex."

I turned to introduce Elizabeth, but he got in first. "Miss Bicester, I am pleased to meet you again."

"I am now Mrs Urquhart, Eddie."

I'm sure I detected a slight disappointment in his expression but it vanished quickly. "My congratulations to you both."

The use of his first name caused a devilish thought to come into mind. For I remembered Elizabeth had been out with someone locally and he looked like someone she might fancy. I asked, "Do you come from Horsham, sir?"

"Why, yes. But I do not believe we have met. Has my reputation preceded me? I hope it is not too derogatory." he replied with a gentle smile to both of us.

Just then I felt an excruciating pain in my right foot. Elizabeth is not a heavy girl by any means, and I generally regard her as quite light-footed. However, her heel, which was now grinding into the top of my patent leather shoe, felt like a steel pin. My hunch was right. He was an ex-flame. Nevertheless, despite the pain, I thought I could get a little more mileage out of this opportunity to dig into her past before my foot was totally broken.

"Not at all, sir," feeling the heel pressing quite hard. "Elizabeth's father mentioned you in passing in connection with the borrowing of a carriage. Ow!"

A sharp nail from my nearest and dearest was now driving into my wrist.

"Are you alright, sir?"

"Yes. These shoes are rather tight."

He looked down just before Elizabeth could remove her heel. I noticed she was a little pink in the face.

"You have my sympathy. "I prefer a pair of boots with armoured caps. I find them essential in certain situations." Then looking at us both with an obvious knowing smile he smoothly changed the subject. "Now where are my manners?

149

Who is this charming lady?"

"If you ask me, I might tell you," said Jill sweetly.

He turned and looked at her, slightly open mouthed then back to me, "Does the lady usually speak before she's introduced?"

"Yes, she does," said Jill before I could reply. Then finishing off her absinthe, she handed him the empty glass, and asked, "Would you mind getting me another? I believe it's not polite for a girl to get her own drink and even less polite to allow her to stand with an empty one."

As he stood there looking at the glass and her in some surprise, she said, "Oh, I'm sorry. Where are my manners. Get yourself one as well. If you ask old Smethers nicely he'll fill them to the top."

He turned to me in wonder so I said, "May I introduce my sister, Miss Jillian Urquhart?"

He grinned and nodded as though everything was explained and said, quite kindly, "Ah, so you are Miss Urquhart. I am most pleased to meet you for I am told by Henry that you often bring refreshment to a dull party."

This man had class. I was taking notes.

He then extended his hand to kiss hers.

"Ooh! You smoothie. Let me take my glove off. You don't want fluff in your whiskers." And she peeled off her glove: a crime of such magnitude in Elizabeth's society that I expected it to be reported in the next edition of the Tatler.

The shock of seeing her naked arm caused him to drop his monocle as well, luckily it missed her glass. Nevertheless he held his nerve and gave her hand quite a long kiss.

When he finally let go, she said, "Whew! Well, you passed the first test. Let's go and get smashed and if you have some good stories, maybe you'll pass the second test as well. Come on. Don't be shy." And before he could protest, she put her arm through his and dragged him off to help him refill their glasses.

I turned to Elizabeth, who was holding a small lace handkerchief to her mouth to hide her laughter. "You two are incorrigible!" she whispered.

"My foot really hurts!"

"Good! Fancy discussing a lady's reputation in front of a former acquaintance."

"So, he was your ex-boyfriend from Horsham. Seemed quite nice. Glad I didn't have to compete with him."

"Are you jealous James? I'm flattered."

"Not a bit! What a suggestion. Where you in love with him?"

"Ha! So, you are! But some things should not be discussed. I do not enquire of you regarding your previous lady friends. Do I?"

"You don't have to. You get all that from Jill during your so-called afternoon teas with her."

"I confess the subject has come up in passing." She said trying not to laugh again. Then looking across the room at no one in particular, "And I know why you did not pick up that lady called Jane from that party."

"Damn! Do I have no secrets? That was a bad evening. I've learnt not to try and manage two girlfriends at once."

"I am glad to hear it. However, having now seen your sister in action, so to speak, with poor Eddie, I now understand, when you first met me at that cricket match at Hamgreen what you were expecting from a lady. In the circumstances, you behaved very well."

"Thank you. And so did you. Now," I said, noticing her shocked look and changing the subject quickly, "let's go and talk to Wells and see which one he is."

151

Chapter Fifteen

E,

How well I remember the evening that Edward Ponsonby proposed to me! I was eighteen had just come out. He had visited with my cousin Henry twice and I confess I became quite infatuated by his attention, kindness and manners. I think my cousin thought we would be a good match. However, I had declined his offer because I wanted to take full advantage of my opportunity to go up to Girton. Certain friends, not surprisingly, regarded me as a fool for although in James' time, a woman can be a wife and a student, in my day such opportunities for a young lady living in the country were rare and a proposal from someone who is agreeable and with monies to support a wife, as Eddie was, was even rarer. I was therefore surprised that my father did not take great exception to my decision. Though later, I realised why. Eddie and I corresponded for a brief period after I went up until distance and distraction separated us.

After my marriage to James, my father mentioned that he had found my correspondence and asked if I wished to keep them. I declined and I could see from his expression that he had used it as a little test of my love for James. Nevertheless, I could not resist enquiring of what had become of Eddie and discovered that he had joined the army, not due to unrequited love, thankfully, but because he wished to see a little of the world.

And now here he was again. Except he was now ensconced in a corner with James' sister where I imagine in the next hour or so he would learn more about life than he had during all of his experiences of the Empire.

J,

As I hobbled over to Mr Wells, Elizabeth's father joined him and grabbed my arm.

"Excuse me, James, but if you have finished your introductions, I would like you both and Mr Wells to come to the Conservatory."

Seeing no reason why not, we followed him through a small door into the glass panelled room. It was real Victorian, complete with palms and aspidistras and I promised myself yet again that if I ever got rich I would build one just like it for us.

The large red-orange globe of Mars still occupied a corner of the room and the brass telescope through which I had previously seen the canals of Mars stood on the mahogany table by the window. When we were assembled, Elizabeth's father said, "I understand from Mr Wells that you have succeeded in joining time again, but unfortunately, it has caused an instability."

Before we could question what he meant or what we'd done, he went over to the door and closed it. Immediately the room felt oppressive and I took Elizabeth's hand. Inexplicably, the light through the windows from the garden began to fade.

"I think we will soon need some more light," he said and proceeded to light a taper and ignite two oil lamps on the sideboards.

The room grew darker until only the lamps illuminated us.

Elizabeth's hand was holding mine quite tightly now.

"I think we are ready, Mr Wells. Shall we begin?" said her father.

"Yes. As you saw this evening, Isabel and I have been

reunited at last. However, neither of us are from this time. In this world, I was married to Isabel. Then I divorced her and ran off with another woman. In my world, I never married her."

"But what about all your books? Did you write them?" I said.

"I did. However, the important question that confronts us here is, which world is this house in?"

"What do you mean? Surely it exists in all worlds." I said.

"I do not believe it does."

"But we have been in different worlds and always found it here." said Elizabeth.

"That does not imply that it exists in every world." said Wells.

"I don't understand." I said. "We know it's outside time because it's always 1895 here." I said.

"But surely it cannot only exist in 1895?" said Elizabeth, "I was born and brought up here."

"It is the house, Mrs Urquhart, that is in stasis." said Wells. "It does not arrest the passage of time for the people within. The effect is embodied only in the structure of the house. Time itself does not exist for the house itself. It is a space between time."

"You mean time flows around and through the house." I said beginning to get an idea of what he was talking about.

"Yes. But it is more complicated. All time lines are bent in its vicinity and join at a moment in 1895 then diverge again."

"So, no matter which world's time-line you are travelling in, if you come to this place you will find yourself in 1895." I said.

"Yes. That is how I understand it."

"But, I must press you," said Elizabeth, looking as puzzled as me, "Is it physically on the Earth? If, as you say, time is distorted here, what has happened to space? Oh, this is difficult. I mean is it really on the Earth or is it actually in another place?" said Elizabeth.

"You mean does it exist somewhere else?" I said, trying to follow her track.

"Yes. Imagine, once upon a time this house or whatever it is, existed on, say, another planet. Then something distorted the space around it and that piece of space along with this place was pushed or flung to another part of the universe. Like here."

"Hell's bunnies! What did you have for breakfast? That would suggest, somewhere else is a hole in space where it once existed. However, that doesn't explain why are we here? And more importantly, why has it gone dark outside?"

"Because this space is moving and the house within it is travelling back to where it came." said Wells.

"You mean we're trapped here?" said Elizabeth.

"I would suggest that no one goes outside at the moment."

I went over to the window. It was black.

I turned and said. "Just one thing. Do you know at what date in 1895 this house exists?"

"Inside here it is the 13th of March. The day the apparatus of Mr Tesla was destroyed by you, Mr Urquhart."

Chapter Sixteen

E.

If an orange glow had not appeared in the window at that moment I think James would have given Mr Wells a severe blow. It was more than a little unfair to accuse James of causing the house to move after bringing the world back together again.

We watched in silence and with not a little trepidation as the orange ball, for that is what it was, swelled until it filled the window. I was mesmerised and felt as if we were drifting in a hot air balloon, rather than in our house.

"It's Mars! Look there's the Marina Valley." James shouted.

The great scar which crossed almost a third of the Martian surface grew larger and larger. In the shadows of its great canyons which passed across our view, wisps of grey cloud rose and turned white, evaporating as they caught the weak sunlight.

The valley began to slowly rotate until the three Tharsis volcanoes with Mons Olympus behind slowly rose over the horizon. As we moved closer I saw green vegetation spreading out from the canyons into the surrounding orange desert. Closer and closer we travelled as if in a dream until with a sharp jolt I was brought back from my reverie and found ourselves on the surface looking out over a dark green and orange canyon. For a moment, there was silence as we stared at the tableau before us then James exclaimed – an idea I had come to conclude but could not believe.

"Good God! Does this mean the house and all its occupants are now on Mars?"

I suddenly thought of Flory and rushed to the door. Mr Wells stopped me with a swift push of his hand.

"We do not know what might be there. Let me look." And he turned the handle and slowly opened the door, He slammed it back within a second.

"It is Mars out there. We are detached from the house!" then with a heartfelt cry, "I have lost Isabel!"

"Calm yourself, Mr Wells." said my father, though I could see from his eyes that he was having difficulty following his own advice. "Perhaps the house did not come with us. And they are all safe."

With no understanding of what was required of us we gazed motionless at the Martian landscape. By now, most of the clouds in the canyon had risen and dispersed to reveal deep channels, lush with green vegetation. As the sun climbed higher in the sky, rays of light began to penetrate the deepest recesses, revealing by their bright glints the traces of a river.

James said, "For a moment I thought we had been transferred back to before the cataclysm. But I think we are somewhere in our time. That's new vegetation."

"Does that mean we can go outside?" I said.

"I doubt it. I don't think the Mars surface will have our oxygen content and the atmosphere on a planet half our size will be far too low. We'd boil in seconds."

"Then we are trapped in our glass bubble!"

"Possibly not. There must be some reason why we are here."

Then he turned to my father. "Have you seen this effect before or did it just start today? I got the impression when you invited us in here you were expecting something."

"On several occasions the sky has dimmed to almost blackness over the last few weeks. But normality always returned within a few minutes. I must admit on the first two I presumed we were about to receive a violent thunderstorm and thought when the light returned it had passed us by."

"Had it happened today before we arrived?"

"Yes. We were in here when the phenomenon returned. For some reason, I did not hear the doorbell. Then I heard the loud banging on the door. By the time I arrived at the front entrance you had gone and I surmised whoever had called had turned to the tradesman's entrance."

"I hope we are not the cause of this nightmare." I said.

"Wouldn't be surprised if we are," said James, still looking a little dejected from Mr Wells' accusation. "I reckon, from what you say, there was already instability here in space-time and our arrival from the future caused a twitch which pushed it over the top. The interesting thing to me though is that if the space occupied by this house or conservatory sprang back to where it came from, then your house originated on Mars."

"A good hypothesis, Mr Urquhart," said Mr Wells. "And your implication is that it was built by the Martians?"

"Possibly. Though I've no evidence for it."

"Then just coincidence?"

I could not ascertain whether he was questioning James' statement or challenging it. I could see James was becoming frustrated again with Mr Wells. One never knows whether he is participating or just guiding us to a conclusion of which he is already aware.

"Yeah," replied James, shrugging his shoulders, "Just coincidence like everything else that's happened to us. Except I don't like coincidences. I prefer cause and effect. Such as every time something strange happens, the Martians seem to be involved. And you too, Wells, by the way."

I could see his point although the reason was nowhere apparent. I tried to gather my thoughts or, to use James' phrase when faced with a conundrum, tried to use both neurons. Unfortunately, I discovered they were both fast asleep and would not be woken.

However, Mr Wells, as usual, managed to raise them from their slumber. "Your house, or the site on which it exists, has been known to the Martians for thousands of years. Whether it was they, or a natural phenomenon, that caused the anomaly I do not know but I know they utilised its existence to create their primary portal to Earth."

"Thanks, Wells." said James, his anger rising again. "You let us try and figure things out first and then when we've all but given up in despair, you throw in the missing bit of the jigsaw."

"It is only by thinking through a process until all that is impossible has been rejected, that the mind is ready to receive the correct solution and act accordingly."

"So, why don't you do it all yourself instead of involving us?" I grabbed James' hand to try and calm him but he ignored it. "Oh yes. I remember. Unlike us, you can't travel through time."

Mr Wells was unflappable in his reply, "You see? Your reply is an example of how my process works?"

Heaven help Isabel, I thought, when she comes to argue with him.

I said, "Sir! You may not realise it, but by your choice of words we perceive you are goading us! Please desist!"

"I apologise. But humans, I find, have limited capabilities in discovering truth and my method is designed to transcend those capabilities."

"Jeeze! Don't tell me you're not human, Wells?" said James.

"I have no idea. I sometimes wonder. As I'm wondering why there is a Martian on the sideboard next to the lamp."

J.

Four heads turned at once and stared. It didn't move. As

usual, Elizabeth and I sought and grabbed each other's hand. I have no idea why we always do this when we're shocked or frightened. It never changes the situation. No doubt Wells will have a reason for it, but I prefer Elizabeth's: it is a comfort.

Its gossamer wings were already shimmering. Automatically my eyes were drawn to the small oval recess in its forehead which I'd concluded long ago was used for some form of telepathic communication. The room blurred. I tried to resist what was coming but I knew it was like fighting to remain conscious just before you go under from an anaesthetic.

The other three had now become grey ghost-like wraiths. And then, we all vanished! I mean really disappeared, including me. I saw nothing. I wasn't there! Then slowly, the grey wraiths returned and grew in form. I could smell damp grass. Then the sound of rustling leaves above. Another moment and the four of us found ourselves standing in a patch of vegetation. As my eyes grew accustomed to the darkness I saw what I was standing in.

"These look like cabbages! Where are we? Is this what Martians eat, Wells?"

"No!"

"Despite what you said, we seem to be breathing the air with no ill effect," whispered Elizabeth to me.

"Well, we shouldn't be, unless the Martians have altered the fundamental laws of physics."

Then I saw a small lamp on a wall about fifty yards away.

"Let's try and get to that. It might be an entrance to one of the Martian caverns."

We walked, no, waded, through the vegetation until we stumbled into some form of brambles recognisable by the sharp pain their thorns gave to the flesh.

"God, I hope they're not poisonous." I said.

"And I hope you still have some of the monies Mr Wells

gave you for a new dress. For this one is shredded."

"How many dresses have I ruined?"

"Every adventure you have taken me on... ouch! These thorns! I have a good mind to wear a maid's garments in future."

"Mmh! Nice idea. I bet you'd look quite good in them."

"You are incorrigible!"

"I know. Took your mind of this nightmare for a minute though. Ah! We've reached the edge. Looks like a path. Where's your father? I thought he was following us."

"I am over here by the lamp, Mr Urquhart." A voice called.

When we eventually reached him I said, quite breathless and sore, "How did you get here so quickly? I thought we took the straightest path."

"I believe you did and I see my daughter was fool enough to follow you."

"What path did you take then? It's nearly pitch black."

"I had the advantage of knowing the paths quite well."

"You've been here before, Father?" said Elizabeth, sounding quite annoyed. "You are as bad as Mr Wells for taking advantage of us."

"Do you not recognise it, Elizabeth?" said her father, giving an expression a parent gives to a confused child. "I am surprised. You used to play here a lot."

We both looked at each other and seeing no enlightenment returned to him.

"It is our kitchen garden'"

"The kitchen gardens!" we both yelled.

Elizabeth turned back to me. "Oh, I am such a fool. Why did I not recognise it? There is the old seat by the rose trellises. I blame you, James, for leading me on."

"Rubbish. I'm blaming you for thinking I knew what I was doing. And not knowing your own backyard. By the way, where's Wells? Don't tell me he's disappeared again!"

As if to answer my question there was a rustle in the undergrowth and out he popped, covered in mud.

"I presume by your state, Wells, you applied your own logic and having rejected all possible paths you decided to take the only impassable one."

"That is not amusing, Mr Urquhart."

Well I thought it was funny.

However, now we were all assembled we realised we were faced with the next problem. What or who was on the other side of the door? Was it the house or another door to Mars?

E.

I do worry why we ladies follow men so blindly sometimes. They seem to have skills in avoiding our argument or reason just when we think we have gained advantage. Though when I have questioned James on this, he invariably replies that he only dreams of gaining an advantage over me.

Thankfully when we opened the door and entered, we found ourselves in the kitchen. Unfortunately, the relief of finding myself home was short lived when I regarded myself in the reflection of the window. It was difficult to believe that the ragamuffin before me was the same person who, only an hour ago, had arrived in the drawing room wearing the new and expensive dress James had bought me to replace the previous one consigned to charity after our last adventure. However, as I thought this enterprise was not concluded, I resisted the urge to rush upstairs and change into another. For I reasoned that the expense of charging James for two garments in one evening would meet with some argument which I might not be able to convince him was entirely his fault.

As we walked into the hallway I noticed that the house was rather quiet and it was with some trepidation that we entered the drawing room.

The tableau that confronted us was not quite what I had expected.

Chapter Seventeen

J.

After I had removed all the thorns I could find we entered the drawing room. It was empty, if you did not include my sister lying sprawled across a green silk sofa fast asleep with her head on poor old Ponsonby's shoulder. To give him his due, he didn't look very comfortable with this opportunity. When he saw me, he immediately got up and straightening his jacket, said, "Excuse me, Mr Urquhart. I hope you do not think I have taken advantage of your sister, but it seems my conservation has had a rather soporific effect on her."

Poor chap. He was so polite.

"Don't worry, Mr Ponsonby. I think you will find her conversation with the absinthe has caused her predicament."

"Thank you." He said, visibly relieved by my answer. "I must say she has a strong constitution for the stuff. I hope you will not think that I led her on, for while she was awake, we had the most delightful and interesting discussion."

"In what way?"

"She claims she came here in a horseless carriage in under half an hour from Chichester and where she lives they have devices that can access all the knowledge of the world."

"Oh!"

"She then proceeded to show me such a device. It was a small black tablet. But unfortunately, she was unable to operate it. I fear the absinthe may have got the better of her and influenced her thinking."

As if to answer this, my sister stirred and putting her arms around his legs pulled him involuntarily back onto the sofa and snuggled up close to him again.

With some difficulty, he extricated himself from her as politely as possible then said, "I think Sir, your sister is ready to retire."

"Agreed. Do you want arms or legs?"

Under Elizabeth's instruction, to ensure some form of modesty prevailed, we proceeded to carry Jill up to her bedroom where having laid her on the bed, Elizabeth said, "I will put her to bed, gentlemen if you don't mind."

We didn't and left her to it.

After about half an hour, when I was nearly dozing off, Elizabeth came into our room.

"How is she?"

"I would not wish to have her head in the morning."

"Nor me. Do you think Ponsonby will recover? He seems such a nice man."

"I am sure he will. Though he may wonder what family I have married into. Now move over so I can have your warm patch. That infernal garden has given me a chill."

She undressed, got into bed and snuggled up close. "What a day. How is your foot?"

"I've suddenly forgotten all about it."

E.

The next morning before we assembled for breakfast, James and I explored the house and the kitchen garden to try to convince ourselves that the night before was just a terrible dream caused by the absinthe. We decided to try the garden first as James said he needed the air. Presuming he had drunk to excess I teased him a little but he replied that he had kept his measure but stupidly shared a cigar with Eddie before retiring. He was convinced that after his first and last inhalation of the weed, his lungs had collapsed, and he feared they would never recover unless he convalesced by the sea for at least a year. I said, with little sympathy, that I also hoped the weed had caused an amnesia of any gems he might have gathered regarding Eddie and me.

The smile he gave me in reply was not reassuring.

When we entered the garden, the muddy trail across the cabbage patch and the broken blackberries leading to the door quickly convinced us that the previous evening's experiences were not the result of befuddled minds. However, everything in the house gratifyingly seemed to be in its place until we turned the corner towards the Conservatory.

It was not there! Instead, we were confronted with a smoothly sculptured, chalk-white, earthen concave floor open to the sky.

"My God! Part of the house has been uprooted James! How did we survive?"

"With luck." He said, looking as shocked as me. "We could've been standing in the doorway and split in half. God, I feel a bit dizzy thinking about it. Let's go have some breakfast. I think I can force a slice of toast down me."

Mr and Mrs Wells were in the parlour drinking tea having had their breakfast.

"I trust you have all recovered from last night?" inquired Mr Wells, who had a large red scratch on his cheek.

"Yes, thank you." James said. But my mind was elsewhere for Jill and Eddie were not present. As I thought of how to introduce the topic of their whereabouts as delicately as possible, without showing any residual affection for Eddie, and trying to remember that Jill was my best friend, I was, as usual in this area, pre-empted by James.

"So, where are the two love-birds? Don't tell me wily old Ponsonby sneaked back upstairs for a bit of the old 'how's your father'?"

My best description for Mrs wells' reaction to this statement was that she threw a fit. "How dare you, Mr Urquhart? Your remark is entirely unfounded and a slur on Captain Ponsonby who is an upright and honourable man."

"I'm sure he is - in the barracks with his mates."

"I will ignore that. For your information, Captain Ponsonby left last night by horse, kindly lent by your wife's father. I am sure you will find your sister is as virtuous now as when she arrived."

"On that point I cannot but agree, Mrs Wells." said James, spluttering out a mouthful of toast.

And then as if on cue, the topic of conversation arrived in the parlour, still in my nightdress, and clutching her head.

"Could someone draw the curtains? That sun is blinding."

James dutifully half closed the curtains. "How you doing, Sis?"

"As well as can be expected. How's Ponsonby? I vaguely remember him holding on to my legs for some reason."

"He was helping me carry you upstairs."

"What? Oh dear. I've done it again. Wait! He's not still in my bed, is he? I didn't look."

"No. He went home last night. You'll be pleased to know that your virtue is still intact."

"Thank God! I didn't want to find I'd woken up with one of Elizabeth's ex-boyfriends. Oh! Hello, Elizabeth. Didn't see you there. Sorry!"

"It is of no consequence. I do not have any claim over him." I said, hoping the colour I felt on my face was not noticed as I wondered what intimate details regarding my past had been discussed between them.

Luckily, at this point, Mrs Wells rose from the table in a huff and left the room, leaving us with Mr Wells who was studiously regarding the remains of his poached eggs.

"What's wrong with her?" said Jill, trying to pour a cup of tea with a rather shaky hand.

"Her husband has run off with some woman. Remember?" said James, completely missing the reason for Mrs Wells' sudden departure from the parlour.

"Gosh! Did you run off with her as well Mr Wells, you naughty boy. Who is she?" said Jill waving her spoon in his general direction.

I will not record the conversation that followed but suffice to say that James, after a few words from me, did sterling work in bringing his sister back on to the track and mollifying Mr Wells.

J.

Once I'd been reminded and agreed that the mix up on who was who, and who did what, was all my fault, a fragile peace was restored.

"So, what happened last night, Wells?" I asked, trying to get back onto a safer ground.

"It was as you suggested. Part of space snapped and catapulted a portion of the house back to Mars."

"OK." I said, not getting anywhere as usual, "Let's try another tack. We know this house exists but where, actually, is it?"

"It is here."

"Yes. We know that, Wells. But where is 'here'?"

"It is not anywhere. You cannot point to a place in our Universe where it exists."

"But we're standing in it!" said Jill, "Look!" And to prove her point banged the wall with her fist.

"That does not prove that it is here in Sussex." said Wells.

"As long as Sussex is outside when I leave, that'll be good

enough for me," she said.

"But is the remains of this house still in 1895?" said Elizabeth.

"I'll check the internet." I said, "Looks like it. No signal whatsoever."

"What about the conservatory?"

"Let's have a look."

We all rose. Some more shakily than others and trooped off to the door leading to the conservatory. On opening, it looked out onto the chalk-white ground, just as we had found when outside. Jill stared open-mouthed at us all. I tried my phone.

"Nothing. Though that doesn't mean time hasn't changed here."

"God! What about the car, Jim?" said Jill, "How are we going to get home? I can barely crawl to the front door."

We went back through the house to the front door and looked out. No car to be seen.

"But we came in by the garden." said Elizabeth. "Remember on that previous occasion when depending on which door we left or entered, time changed?"

"This is getting like Heinlein's 'Crooked House'," I said.

"Where is that?" said Elizabeth.

"It's a fictional story about a bloke who tried to build a four-dimensional house and it kept on collapsing and reforming in other dimensions. I think he and the house eventually disappeared."

I suddenly realised what I'd said and by the expression on the others' faces they had had the same idea. Jill got in first.

"Get out of this house! Run!" and we followed her. As we ran through the kitchen, Lilly, who was washing up and humming a tune was quite surprised when Elizabeth grabbed her hand and pulled her out into the garden with us.

Avoiding the brambles this time, we all ran around to the

169

front where I was relieved to find my car.

"Thank God for that," said Jill and sat down on the porch step nursing her head.

"I think we should go home now before another anomaly occurs." said Elizabeth.

"Yes," I said, "But just a minute! Where's Wells?"

"Did he not come out of the house?" said Elizabeth.

"I wasn't watching," I said. "Did you see him, Lilly?"

But she wasn't listening. She was looking at my car.

"Is this your carriage, Mr Urquhart?"

I couldn't lie. It was fifteen-foot-long, green and nothing like a Victorian carriage. "Yes," I said.

"How do you attach the horses?"

I knew that was coming.

"It uses a steam engine, Lilly. A state of the art device which James has designed and built for me," said Elizabeth.

"Well I never, Lizzy! What is the world coming to? Can I have a ride, Mr Urquhart?"

"We are pressed for time, Lilly," said Elizabeth.

But I couldn't let her miss out so I said she could have a go around the courtyard.

Afterwards she said, "Cor, Lizzy! What a catch you have. You look after him. He'll see you right."

"I will try to remember that, Lilly."

"But why were you all rushing out of the house?"

"We are late for an engagement."

"Then I must not stop you."

And she turned back and vanished through the garden wall! Literally through the wall as though it wasn't there.

Elizabeth grabbed my arm "What shall we do? We must go back! My father is in there as well."

"I'm not going back," said Jill, "Not if the house is going to collapse."

I agreed.

"But I cannot leave my father if the house is in danger, James."

I wish I hadn't brought up Heinlein. For before I could stop her, she stepped back and vanished through the wall as well!

Jill and I looked at each other.

"Families, eh, Jim. You can't compete with them. I presume you're not abandoning the love of your life. Even though she's more worried about her dad than you."

She looked at my face and then took pity on me and held my hand.

"Come on. Let's go and rescue the damsel in distress."

"Thank you. I owe you one. Just one thing though. There's another reason for not going back to Chichester."

"What's that?"

"Look at what you're wearing."

She looked down and realised with horror she was still in one of Elizabeth's nightdresses. It was one of those white winter ones normally associated with the inmates of a sanatorium, designed to keep a girl warm and not to emphasise the form of her body.

"Great! I've excelled myself, haven't I? Even by my standards. Gone out partying, got blotto and next morning found wandering home in someone else's nightgown. Whole new standard for the walk of shame."

She saw my hand going to my pocket.

"If I see you get your phone out for a photo, or ever even mentioning this to Sean, you're dead."

I slowly raised both my hands to show they were empty.

She said, "Yeah, I believe you. Just one thing though."

"What's that? You want to see Ponsonby again?"

"No! Have you got any aspirin?"

Chapter Eighteen

E.

I went through the wall into a garden of hollyhocks and fuchsias which rose around me higher than a house. Between them, long tendrils of petunias, supported magically by nothing but themselves waved in the soft breeze. As I stood there in wonder an almost overpowering fragrance of wallflowers wafted over me. I was enchanted. My eyes closed in reverie. I wanted James to live here with me for ever.

And then I remembered! James!

What had I done! I had abandoned him to save my father!

My Victorian morals enveloped me. What would he say? Would he think my father came before him? I felt the panic of the dilemma rising and took a step back which to my surprise caused me to float into a dense clump of petunias. I tried disentangling myself from them, but I became more entwined. Eventually though brute force I broke their strands and freed myself. However, when I rose to walk again I almost cartwheeled. What magic was this that had released me from my earthly bounds? Then as I slowly straightened myself and smoothed my skirts removing petunia flowers from my belt and shoes, I saw a gravel path between a row of fuchsia. With some caution, I moved towards it, one slow step at a time. Yet even with control I found myself gliding and slipping. At one point, feeling myself falling, I grabbed a hollyhock, but it snapped and came down with me and in the process released two peacock butterflies which inexplicably alighted on my hair!

By now I was nearly beside myself. Nevertheless I resolved to persevere and follow the path the best I could for I could see no other escape.

Step by step I went forward through this enchanted garden expecting at any moment a phantasmagorical creature to poke its head through the hollyhocks. But try as I might I could not control my gait and danced as if I was a fairy flitting from flower to flower.

After fifty yards or so, I could not measure it, I came out of the foliage on to a green lawn bound on three sides by a hundred-foot-high yew hedge above which two moons hung in the orange sky. I then knew where I was, though how, I could not reason. In the far boundary of the lawn, I espied an arch. I walked or should I say I bounded over to it but unfortunately, halfway across the lawn I caught a foot in a croquet hoop and found myself bowling over and over until I landed sprawled against the yew hedge. When I rose and gathered my wits and skirts I noticed a frog regarding me not three feet away. I still do not know why a vision of James dressed as one came to me at that moment. But it helped to quench my fears a little. I carefully looked through the arch and saw a rose covered veranda beside a house overlooking a lush deep green canyon which stretched to the horizon. Within the veranda, sitting in wicker chairs taking afternoon tea, were my father and Mr and Mrs Wells!

I literally danced uncontrollably towards them. When I arrested my flight by grabbing and half swinging around a pillar of the veranda, my father, without the slightest concern for my welfare said, "Oh. Hello Lizzy. I thought you had left for home. Would you like some tea? I can get Lilly to make a fresh pot." said

"I did not return for tea father!" I said with some anger rising. "I returned to see if you were safe!"

He then noticed my expression and replied as one does to a child. "Oh, we are perfectly safe here, Lizzy. Why don't you join us and watch the Martian sunset?"

"Forgive me, but for some reason which now escapes me, on impulse I abandoned my husband to look for you."

"Oh, I don't think you have. I'm sure he will be here in a minute or two. Provided he takes the right path."

Before I could reply, I heard in the distance a strange scream. I turned in the direction of the sound and saw to my horror a white phantom rise above the hollyhocks. It then slowly turned and fell back down again. My blood ran cold.

J.

We found ourselves in some strange garden with flowers and plants stretching almost up to the sky. Elizabeth had vanished.

Jill said, "Where the hell are we now? And what are those two moons doing up there?"

I looked up. "It's Mars."

"We're on Mars! Just like that? No jumping about like a gibbering gibbon on realising we've just gone through a wall and ended up million miles away on a planet where we can miraculously breath the air?"

"The Martians are rehabilitating their planet."

"Oh, that's alright then. Pardon me for questioning what I'm seeing and breathing."

I cast my eyes around trying to guess where Elizabeth had gone.

"Any idea which way she went?"

"Who? No. For some reason, I totally forgot about your wife for a moment. And why are these hollyhocks a hundred feet tall?"

"It's the gravity. Try jumping."

"Have you lost your marbles again Jim? I'm going back."

And before I could stop her, she attempted to run back to

the wall and flew through the air and straight through it.

After about a minute she materialised back through the wall.

"Ok, Ok. I've got it now." she said, straightening Elizabeth's now rather muddied and torn nightdress. "Just another normal day flitting about in time and space with you idiots. What do we do now?"

"Get out of this vegetation."

After about ten minutes of stumbling about, we eventually and surprisingly found the beginning of the path we had just created through the hollyhocks.

"I thought you were the boy scout who never gets lost. Do you have a Plan B?" she said.

"Jump as high as you can."

"What? Oh, I see! Give me a lift."

It's not often you get to throw your fully-grown sister in the air. But after three attempts aided by the weak gravity she eventually saw the edge."

'Wow! That was fun, especially the somersault. Oh! Oh!...'' her face changed colour, "Wait a minute I don't feel well. God I'm going to be sick!"

When she recovered, she said "I don't think Elizabeth's going to want her nightie back. Ugh! Never let me drink absinth again."

"Are you OK sis?"

"Yea. Nothing but a day in bed wouldn't cure. It's this way. Follow me."

Surprisingly, the path was only a few yards away and we followed it across a field and through a gap in a hedge. Jill was first to go through. The scream I heard from the other side of the hedge was quite loud. When I entered, Jill was knelt on the ground cradling Elizabeth.

I rushed over. A mistake, for I sailed past them, without a hello or goodbye, and landed on a veranda where to my surprise the Wells and her father were sitting. Oh, and also what looked like what might have been a few seconds before I arrived, a well laid out table for afternoon tea.

I was just in the process of getting up to make introductions and apologises when someone or something slammed into me, bowled me over again and smothered me in kisses and nearly crushed me to death in the process.

"Oh James! Will you ever forgive me?"

"If you're going to do that every time you leave me, you can run off whenever you like. What happened to you?"

"She thought I was a ghost," said Jill.

"Why?" I said, "Oh yes, I see. You look like......"

"Shall we leave it there Jim?"

It was then that I noticed her father and the Wells staring at us. I've found the best tactic in this situation is to pretend nothing has happened. Thankfully, Elizabeth's father, was of a similar mind and even more thankfully, Mrs Wells was lost for words.

When we had rearranged the table and chairs and Lily had come out and replaced the china, he said, "Now you three, please sit down. Take some tea and enjoy the sunset, for it will not last much longer."

We did as we were told, for it was, as I regarded the landscape before me, the most perfect thing to do.

As the small orange sun approached the horizon, clouds of vapour, their tops orange in the sunlight began to form in the valley. I felt my mind relax for the first time in days and I sunk deeper into the chair. I noticed Wells and her father continued to sip their tea as if this scene was the most natural thing in the world and it occurred to me that this may not have been their first time here. I said. "Do you come here often Mr Bicester?"

He preferred that to Squire Bicester.

177

"Yes," he said, without batting an eyelid, "Since the anomaly, the garden does seem to flit about. Mr Wells and I have tried to calculate the frequency of occurrence but it seems to be random. Though I must say it is often at sunset."

"And then what happens?" trying to keep up the pretence that this was a normal conversation.

"Oh. After about an hour or so, there is a slight shimmer and we return home."

"Is that all? And the house?"

"It seems quite happy with it. Though we have lost the Conservatory I'm afraid."

I didn't really care. I sat back and returned to watching the sunset. Jill had fallen asleep in her chair, still in the remains of Elizabeth's night dress. Isabel had her usual expression of one whose society had collapsed around her, and it was all my fault. Wells was trying to fold a paper napkin into some form of airplane or perhaps another time machine for all I knew.

The colours of the foliage in the valley were fading fast in the spreading twilight. Elizabeth moved her chair closer to me and gentle entwined her fingers in mine. Her father noticed and gave me a smile which I returned then he rang a small bell on the table. Lilly appeared and he asked, "Could you bring a couple of lamps? I think everyone is staying out here for a while"

She returned shortly with two and hung them on the trellis. Then as the sun sunk below the horizon a soft warm breeze blew a fragrance of honeysuckle and roses over us and suddenly the sky was full of stars.

I languidly reached over to the table and took another cake and as I shared it with Elizabeth a silvery light cast our shadows upon the lawn. We both looked up and saw our own Moon rising above the trees.

We were nearly home.

Then just as I was drifting off I felt a hand gently touch me on the shoulder and turning, thinking it was Elizabeth, saw Lilly out of the corner of my eye. She seemed a little pensive.

"Excuse me Mr Urquhart."

I said, "Yes Lilly?" expecting either the offer of more cake or the news that there was none left.

"I did not want to disturb you, Mr Urquhart after your day but there is a Mr Tesla at the door who is most insistent on seeing you. He seems a little agitated."

Part III

A Ship in the Night

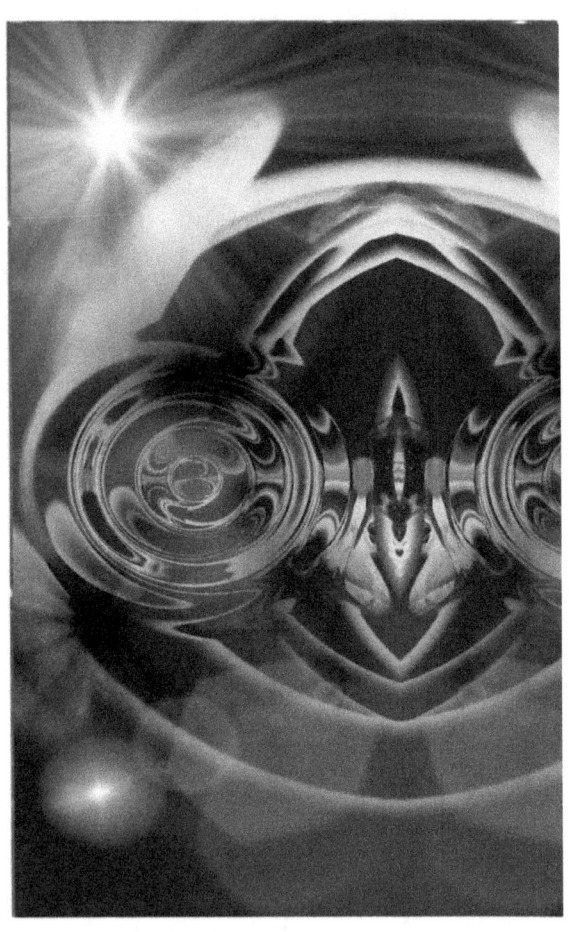

Chapter Nineteen

E.

It is still difficult to describe the pandemonium that ensued on the announcement of Mr Tesla's presence; for the last and only time we had met him we had destroyed his electrical apparatus and in the process whisked ourselves away into I don't know when or where without a goodbye or adieu. I could only presume he would be rather annoyed and would be demanding some recompense. James was of a similar opinion and suggested, following Tacitus dictum that we run for his carriage. I must admit I found favour with this and was about to accompany him when without any introduction, Mr Tesla appeared at the kitchen door. He was dressed in a dark grey coat unbuttoned and still wearing his bowler! Then without a nod of introduction he glanced at us and on espying James exclaimed, "Mr Urquhart! I must have words with you."

Everybody was now standing including Jill who on being awoken from her sleep and I imagined still nursing a sore head reciprocated his lack of manners by demanding to know why he had disturbed a peaceful and tranquil sunset. Her presence and her words put Mr Tesla on the back foot not least because she introduced herself in the tattered remains of my white night dress which in the moonlight betrayed more of her form then would normally be expected of a lady receiving guests.

This, however, fortunately, allowed James to recover.

"Mr. Tesla! I'm so glad to see you. Please sit down and have a cup of tea."

Managing to take his eyes off James' sister on whose body I felt he had gazed a little too long he turned to James. "What?

Oh! Yes! No! I have come to discuss…."

"Just sit down Mr Tesla." said James, pulling over a threadbare wicker chair from the edge of the veranda, "Then we can talk about this in a civilised manner. There are ladies present".

Mr Tesla did not move.

"Ladies!" said James turning to us, "Please sit down otherwise he won't."

Jill and I looked at each other, then at the remains of our clothing and eventually deciding we were to be passed off as ladies took our seats. Though what Mrs Wells thought of us masquerading as such I do not know.

Mr Tesla hesitated for only a moment and then, thankfully remembering his manners, sat down, removed his bowler and placed it on his lap. He was immediately offered and accepted, after a brief hesitation, a cup of tea from Lilly who once again demonstrated her ability to control small children and adults who acted like them and also managed to relieve him of his hat.

She then offered him cake which he also accepted. There then followed an uncomfortable silence while he ate or should I say, devoured it, while we regarded each other.

My father was the first to speak.

"Mr Tesla, I presume that is who you are for you have not introduced yourself, let me present ourselves."

He then took a few moments introducing each of us with a brief resume while Mr Tesla with an occasional nod of acknowledgement continued to scoff his tea and cake. Receiving no reply my father continued as though this conversation was the most natural thing in the world.

"I have heard from James the great things you have done for this world and your work on the advancement of communication."

He had carefully chosen his moment while Mr Tesla's mouth was still full. A trick I recognised from childhood when he wished to gain an advantage over Flory and I during a squabble. On hearing this compliment, I could see Mr Tesla was having difficulty in not immediately responding.

My father took his advantage and continued. "I also understand that you have tried to communicate with Mars. Did you have success?"

Mr Tesla could resist no more and spluttered, "You know of these things? Is it true I will become famous and beat Edison?"

I could see father looked perplexed at this name and he turned to James in the hope of help. "I am sorry, James. But I realise I have walked into a mire of my own making, and I must ask you for assistance."

James luckily took his cue.

"Do you mean the war between AC and DC current Mr Tesla?"

"That is exactly what I mean." said Mr Tesla, gratified that someone had understanding of his meaning, "I am convinced that the generation and transport of electrical current can be made only more efficient with alternating rather than direct current."

"Well, the good news is your right. My whole world is based on alternating currents."

"What world is this?"

"The future."

"You are from the future?"

"I am. The others around you are roughly from this time."

"Then how are you here?"

"That's a long story. But it started with eddies of space-time appearing. One of which I walked into and found myself in the nineteenth century."

"Then time travel is possible!"

"It is. And often too much of it," I said turning to Elizabeth who nodded in agreement.

"But getting back to you alternating currents and Edison, the bad news is that you're going to need some help to sell your idea."

"But I am preparing patents and forming a company! I will show the world my theory is better than Edison's."

I had heard of this Mr Edison before. James told me that the man had once electrocuted an Elephant to demonstrate his power of electricity! I had subsequently 'looked up' this crime on one of his communication devices and was horrified to find an elephant called Topsy was killed in such a manner! However, I was much relieved to find that Mr Edison had nothing to do with it.

James said to him, "I don't want to influence you but you might want to talk to a chap called Westinghouse who I think will be very receptive to your theories and have the money to get it going."

"I will make my own decisions. But to return to why I am here."

"Yes, how did you get here. I thought you were in New York" said James, cleverly twisting the topic of conversation away from his question.

"When you destroyed my machine, I was thrown out of time."

"How do you know?"

"I found myself extended so to speak. I could see the past and future movement of my body. I also saw both of you float away like extruded ghostly apparitions. As you drifted up through the roof I willed myself to follow you and found myself rising as well. We seem to float for ages. Stars appeared and passed me by then, I saw you descend into England and then to a village near the south coast. But just as I tried to see where you had gone the scene changed and I was back in my laboratory."

"I thought it burnt down," said James.

"Yes it did. But that was not caused by you. It was accidently started by workman on a lower floor. All my work was destroyed!"

"I am sorry to hear that," I said feeling relieved that it was not caused by us but I felt that this deviation had progressed far enough and I wished to get to the nub of his visit. I said, "So, why did you wish to speak to my husband?"

He took a last gulp of his tea and putting the cup down hunched forward.

"I have reason to believe that I have contacted Mars or more specifically the inhabitants of that planet."

His voice was quiet and as he spoke his eyes reverently moved as though he was fearful of being overheard. We found ourselves involuntarily hunching forward as well. Though not before both James and I had furtively looked around the veranda for the presence of small white rabbit like creatures

----

J.

Expecting to be beaten up or worse for destroying his machine I was a bit taken aback by what Tesla wanted to talk about. I vaguely remembered some articles on the fringe of the Net about him trying to set up some form of powerful radio wave transmitter to send a signal to Mars.

"What makes you think that you've contacted Mars?" I said, pretending I knew nothing about it.

"I have been constructing a magnifying transmitter."

"A what?" I said.

"It is a more advanced version of my coil transmitter. It is a

187

high-power harmonic oscillator that I intended to use for the wireless transmission of electrical energy."

"Are you trying to conduct electrical power by radio waves instead of cables."

"Yes. I thought this would have required an incredible power source but..."

He hesitated for a moment, again looking around to see if he was being overheard, "I have discovered terrestrial stationary electro-magnetic waves that extend across the earth.

I tried to look as though this was the most important discovery in history and at the same time trying to not give the impression I had no idea what he was talking about.

Then my sister, who I thought had returned to her slumber put me on the spot. "Do they exist Jim?"

"Not that I know of. The earth behaves like a magnet with its iron core but I've not come across it producing magnetic or electro-magnetic waves."

"But it does! Mr Urquhart. The Earth behaved as conductor of very low resistance, and I found it responded to certain frequencies of electrical vibrations."

I'd forgotten what it must have been like in science at the turn of the twentieth century. After two hundred years, the world had broken away from the magical arts and just about consigned them to the realm of charlatans. Even Newton's experiments in astrology and alchemy had been carefully forgotten. Then Rutherford discovered that Thorium could be transmutated into Radon! This was like saying he'd discovered how to turn mercury into gold. His partner Soddy, on discovering what they'd done, apparently exclaimed, "They'll have our heads off as Alchemists!"

This was the world that Tesla lived in. Many of his theories were met with great scepticism if not derision and his attempts to communicate with other planets cost his reputation dear.

But he was not a charlatan. He had immense knowledge of electricity and had a vision for its use.

I said, "You mean… Ah! I see. You think your machine, if it could produce a powerful electrical signal at one of these frequencies, then the earth would resonate with it and provide you with vehicle to transmit your electricity all over the world."

"Precisely I could transmit energy wirelessly over long distances by generating standing waves of electrical energy within the Earth."

"And you intend to use this, er, magnifying transmitter to communicate with Mars?"

"Intend? I have done it Mr Urquhart."

"And what made you think there are Martians there?"

"Why? We know there are Martians there." Looking at me as though I was a simpleton.

This was getting into dodgy ground. I didn't want to admit what we knew about the Red Planet yet otherwise he might clam up. I said, "What evidence have you got?"

"Mr Schiaparelli's observations. Have you not seen them?" he said looking at us rather surprised.

Elizabeth's father helped me out, though I don't think intentionally. "Yes, we have and I am lucky enough to have a Martian globe. Remember James? It was bequeathed to me a few years ago, by my dear old friend Mr William Dawes. Sadly, he is now dead. He did some drawings of Mars for Mr Proctor of the Royal Astronomical Society."

I remembered it well and the adventure that went with it.

"Oh! Of course, yes!" I said, going along with him, "It showed all the canals."

"That is it Mr Urquhart! That is the proof there are inhabitants on Mars," said Tesla. "And it is also supported by Mr Lowell from Arizona who has made similar and independent observations and is convinced that the great canals were built by the inhabitants of Mars and are irrigated by the polar ice caps each season. He has written and published a paper on it."

Elizabeth put her hand on my knee, indicating that she wished to join in and also to signal that she thought she knew what I was doing. "You say that you have communicated with Mars, Mr Tesla. Have you received a reply?"

Tesla withdrew into his secretive self again and whispered. "I have received a series of pulses which by their repetitive nature suggests that it was made by intelligent beings."

At this point, Wells who had been sitting back feigning no interest whatsoever in this conversation said, "And do you have a transcription of this message?"

Expecting Tesla to make some excuse about he had no concrete evidence I was surprised to see him put his hand inside his waste coat and retrieve a small roll of metal foil. He then laid it on the table and proceeded to carefully unroll it. We all moved forward to see what it was.

It reminded me of one of those old pen recorder chart rolls. There was a long black line punctuated by vertical spikes of different sizes. I quickly saw that the spikes although looked random, groups of them repeated themselves at regular intervals.

"I said, "Do you know what it means?"

"No," said Tesla.

"I believe I do."

We all immediately turned to Wells who then produced a piece of paper from one of his many pockets and unfolded it on the table to show an almost exact likeness of Tesla's graph!

Chapter Twenty

E.

Although I know we do not have control of our own destinies, I like to think that I have some influence. Mr Wells seems to take great delight in ensuring that James and I do not.

The two drawings, although I could see were similar, were to me incomprehensible and I noticed from James' expression he was of the same opinion. Mr Wells sensing this proceeded to enlighten us.

"Mr Tesla is right. The earth does produce its own magnetic frequency of which the Martian's are aware. And use it to communicate with Earth.

"But with whom do they communicate Herbert?" said Mrs Wells, not asking what I thought was the obvious question; where did her husband obtain his copy.

He turned to James and I. "You remember the Martians had installed their advanced guard on earth buried underground. Put there thousands of years ago."

"Yes," I said. "How could I forget."

"I believe this is a signal to wake them up and commence the invasion of Earth."

"How can you tell that from this?"

"Have you noticed a certain number of the ratios of the synodic periods of Mars and Venus are almost an exact number of years."

I was about to ask James what this gibberish had to do with meetings of Bishops when to my surprise my father answered.

"Ah! You mean every fourth-year Mars returns to the same position in the Earth's sky almost to the day."

"Yes."

"And Venus every five years?"

"Precisely, Mr Bicester. Now look at these lines."

We looked but still without comprehension.

"It is a like calendar. These lines show the conjunctions of Mars and Earth. The longer the line the nearer Earth is to Mars. These lines repeat every four years. The time when Mars appears in the same place in the firmament."

"And this last line is the longest."

"Yes. When Mars is closest to Earth."

"And when's that?"

Mr Wells looked up at the sky. We immediately followed his gaze and saw rising above the trees the red planet shining quite brightly.

"Are you telling us the Martians are about to invade again," exclaimed James, "We've already been through that hell twice. I thought their underground fleets were destroyed! Elizabeth and I saw one inside the white cliffs."

"But that was in the future. Here it is 1895."

"God!" said James. "When we fought them we had weapons that matched there's. Here you've only got muskets and cannonballs. You'd be wiped out. How long have we got?"

He looked up the sky. Mars had risen higher and the sky was now black.

"I believe about four days plus or minus two.".

He un-nerved me not a little with his calmness and I ventured to try and find out why.

"Have you informed the government of this? For they will need preparation."

"Mr Tesla will provide all the preparation we need."

Mr Tesla looked as perplexed as us.

"In the time cavern, there is a replica of Mr Tesla's

resonance oscillator. A much improved one I believe. We will use it to interfere with the signal."

"You mean block the frequency?" said James.

"Precisely. It should not be difficult. The signal from Mars is rather weak and should easily be countered by Mr Tesla's apparatus."

"Ok. Should be possible in theory. There are just two things that bothers me."

Mr Wells waited.

"First. Where did you get your drawing from?"

"Oh, that was easy. You remember when you all left the cavern."

"Yes. We thought it was a good idea at the time."

"I stayed behind."

"Ah! Is that where you were."

"Yes. I wondered why the oscillator continued to generate sparks."

"Sparks! They were blooming great bolts of lightning!" Said James.

"As you wish. But while I was observing them, I noticed a pattern of smaller discharges and proceed with the aid of my pocket watch to record their frequency. It was not the frequency expected of the oscillator. I did not understand them at first and wanted to find out more, but a particularly large bolt of lightning convinced me that I should leave. I then went back to my lodgings."

"Did you end up in my period?"

"No. I returned via the Coaching Inn and found myself in this time. I spent the night trying to decipher the signal but to no avail. It was only when Mr Tesla mentioned his communications with Mars and produced his foil that I realised what it might mean."

"I do not quite see why you would conclude that it was a

signal for the Martians here on Earth," said my father.

"I admit it is a little tenuous. But I believe that when the Martians detected Mr Tesla's signal they may have thought they were discovered and sent a message to Earth indicating that the next close conjunction would be the best time to commence their invasion."

If he was to be believe, he had reason.

There was a silence for a moment then James spoke.

"Second question. Who's going to block the signal?"

J.

I realised rather quickly that I wasn't going to be able to take the car to Midhurst for although spatially it was only the other side of the garden wall it was over a hundred years in the future; by which time, I imagined we would all be speaking Martian or dead. This left us with the pleasures of late nineteenth century transport and roads.

Luckily, I could depend on my nearest and dearest for she takes to driving a carriage like a duck to water.

I eventually convinced Jill that she should take my car back home in the morning rather than come with us and then we retired to bed. Lilly had somehow in between supplying us with tea and cake had also prepared an extra guest room and ensured that the ensuite facilities had been carefully placed on the side board and under the bed. I sometimes suspected that there were at least a score of hidden servants serving Elizabeth's home, but she assures me that there were only five, if you didn't count gardeners, stable lads and kitchen staff.

I slept fitfully dreaming of trying to operate Tesla's machine and being struck by lightning bolts every time I tried to touch it. I later learnt that at least two of the bolts were Elizabeth slapping me for taking all the bed clothes.

We woke quite early and after a full breakfast shared just between the two of us we went to the stables where Smethers had prepared a dog cart and Wells, Tesla and Elizabeth's father were waiting for us.

I had learnt travelling in an open carriage in this period that wearing a full winter coat, hat and gloves was essential, no matter what the weather and dressed accordingly thanks to the generosity of Elizabeth's father.

However, I was rather annoyed that Wells wasn't coming with us nor shared in his confidence that if we followed Tesla's instruction everything would be alright.

E.

Despite my protestations, Mr Tesla insisted that in the presence of a lady it was a gentleman's duty to drive and handed the reins to James who looked at me then Mr Tesla and mumbled something about a sprained wrist making it impossible for him to take the seat. Although I guessed this was a fabrication to avoid this duty I did not encourage him as I knew, how can I put this politely, that he had limitations in this area. Unfortunately, by the time we arrived at Cocking I was begging James to take the lead for I had quickly discovered, on enquiry of Mr Tesla, after he had removed a finger post and caused a young couple to jump into a ditch that his only knowledge of driving was by way of observation from the top of an omnibus!

Thankfully James eventually acquiesced to my pleading and under my guidance assisted by a rather strong nudge here and there and accompanied by many mutterings concerning the never-ending demands of someone's wife, we arrived safely at Midhurst.

At the Coaching Inn, we handed the horse and cart to a

stable boy after I pressed upon him the need to look after the poor creature properly. I'm sure as it departed it gave me a look that suggested it was wondering why it had deserved to be treated so roughly on the journey. We then took luncheon at the Inn during which there was some considerable argument over my tattered reputation and which route we should take to the cavern. It was eventually agreed that to mollify me, as James put it, that we would proceed to the Cavern via the church so that I would not be seen again taking two men up to the bed chamber!

I do wonder how I find myself in so many situations where my respectability is compromised. Perhaps I think too much about it.

The cavern was as we had left it complete with the modified apparatus. We then both looked askance at Mr Tesla, who we were assured by Mr Wells would provide us guidance but to my consternation he seemed to be regarding us in the same manner.

J.

When I realised Tesla was expecting us to tell him what to do, I was more than a little disappointed. I decided to have a walk around the room until I'd cooled off a bit. It was quiet and the apparatus was sitting there minding its own business without a hint of a spark.

After I had wandered about the cavern for a few minutes trying to look as though I had some plan, Elizabeth said, "Do you think we should switch it on?"

"Yes. I think we should." said Tesla and then they both looked at me. For some reason, I felt this was a little unfair. Seeing by their expressions that they wondering why I was not immediately proceeding with this simple task I said, through gritted teeth. "OK. I'll be the guinea pig again!"

And I went over to the console. I was glad I still had my coat on but for extra protection I put on Elizabeth's father's leather gloves as well.

"James! be careful!"

"Bit late now." I said. Then confirming the cables were in place I pressed the ted button, which in this case was a small lever. For a moment, nothing happened. Then I heard a low frequency hum. I moved back to the edge of the room by the door which I was glad to see was still ajar.

As the machine continued to charge up and a few sparks appeared around the primary coil I suddenly thought and then said rather loudly, "Any idea why I've switched it on?"

I got no answer so I turned it off. Elizabeth later told me when I'd calmed down that the look I gave her and Tesla would have frozen a Troll.

Returning from the console and the machine had become quiet again I said, "OK. Let's have a think about this. Any ideas Tesla?"

Tesla said. "I think I may have been a little hasty in my reply to you. We must first modulate the frequency of the electromagnetic pulses to synchronise with the Martian signal."

"Really! I would never have guessed" I said sarcastically as possible. "And pray tell me how we're going to do that? For as far as I can remember the frequency is dictated by the input frequency, coil size and spark gap width. None of which can be changed while its working without ending up rather crispy!"

"Then we need to change the frequency of the power supply." said Tesla.

"Easier said than done. You'd need a motor generator connected to it. I don't think you're going to find one in

Midhurst even if they've been invented. And if we did, we have no idea what the voltage is of the power supply. It could blow it in seconds."

I felt Elizabeth's hand grasp my arm.

"But why do we need to change the frequency?" said Elizabeth.

We both looked at her. "Carry on." I said.

"Surely the electrical noise generated by this infernal machine would just drown out the signal sent from Mars."

"Only it if were at the same frequency as the carrier wave that brought the Martian signal." I said.

"But it is!" exclaimed Tesla. His eyes lighting up.

"How do you know?" I said, "It could be any frequency."

"The apparatus must be generating at the right frequency already," said Tesla, "for Mr Wells picked up the Martian signal from it. It will interfere with the signal. We must turn it on!"

It made sense. Wells could only have picked it up if it was modulating or amplifying the frequency of the Tesla coil.

However, before I could say anything, Tesla rushed over to the console and pulled the lever.

Within a minute, sparks were flying and I smelt ozone.

"There. We have done it!" said Tesla.

"Maybe," I said grudgingly, carefully watching the streams of plasma form and play around the cavern. "However, as we have already picked up the signal, how do we know the Martians haven't received it already and woken up?"

As if in answer, the walls of the cavern suddenly dissolved and we found ourselves gazing into a much larger cavern within which stretching as far as we could see, rows of sleek green Martian tripod machines.

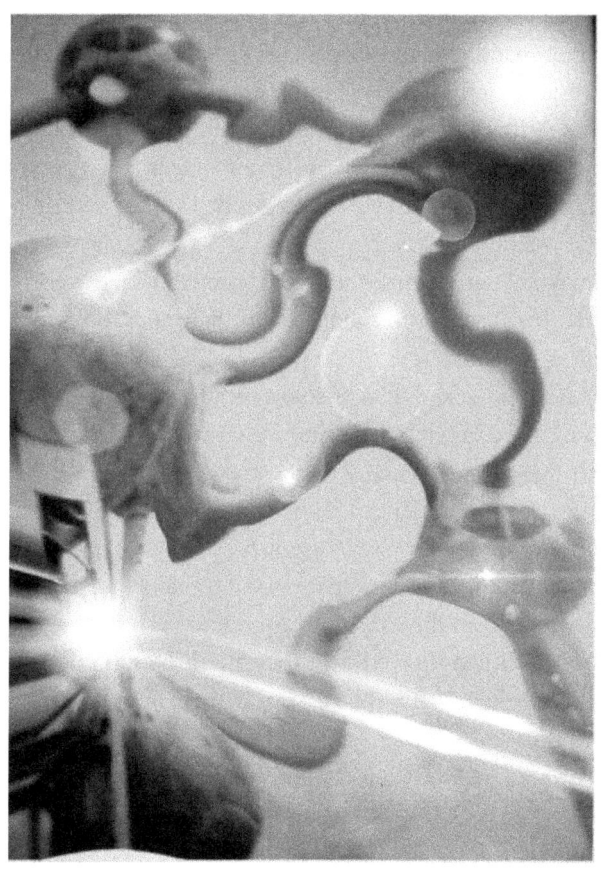

Chapter Twenty-One

E.

To reach a consensus without questioning closely the logic by which it is derived, often results, I have found, in argument if not recrimination. Such a discussion took place shortly after the appearance of the Martian machines on the subject of who agreed to switch on the machine. This lasted a number of minutes, punctuated by bolts of lightning flying across our heads until I decided, for everyone's safety, that we were all to blame for pulling the leaver.

"Thank you," said James. "Now I'm going to turn this damn thing off because I can't cope with lightning bolts and Martians at the same time."

But as he approached the console a great streak of lightning shot from Mr Tesla's apparatus and went through the invisible wall into the cavern where it struck the nearest tripod. The great long arc of light danced between it and the apparatus. I could not comprehend what current passed along its length, but its effect soon became apparent for suddenly a streak of lightning leapt from the Tripod to another!

Blue rivers of light flowed over the tripods bathing them in an iridescent glow. Then the plasma leapt to a third tripod. Then another and another until across the cavern dozens of tripods were joined in strings of blue lightning.

J.

If the Martians were asleep when we turned on Tesla's oscillator, they were definitely awake now for here and there tripods began to move and extend their legs. Half a dozen or so began to rise into the air, but each was caught by fingers of plasma from others on the ground. One by one they glowed and then fell to the ground and landed in crumpled heaps. After few minutes the cavern was littered with smouldering and jerking tripods. Then, I noticed one near us rise up on its three legs and began to walk away from the others to escape the plasma. As it did I saw long tubes extend from its bulbous head. It turned to the nearest tripods and fired from the tubes red beams of light. A beam hit one and it crumpled to the floor, it's head exploding. It obviously thought it could avoid Tesla's plasma by destroying the nearest tripods. Unfortunately, others seeing this began to fire back in defence. Within seconds this caused a chain reaction as just about every Martian tripod decided that everyone else was a threat. It was like watching some mad movie of a robot army which had suddenly decided to exterminate itself.

E.

For a while I was transfixed by this appalling scene of self-destruction until I was brought back to reality by a piece of shrapnel from an exploded Tripod landing still smoking at our feet. Without any discussion on whether to stay or leave we ran for the door and the shelter of the tunnel.

But it was not there! When the walls of the cavern had become transparent the door had disappeared!

We ran around the walls desperately pressing the surfaces in the hope of finding it while lightning bolts flew about us and the Martians continued their suicidal battle. But to no avail. I ran my fingers through my dishevelled hair and felt and heard sparks of electricity. Then the lights went out and once again we saw ourselves in the light from the lightning jets in a moving picture.

James was the first to speak. "Look the Earth and Mars

globes! They're glowing! They must be getting power from the console as well. We can use them to escape"

I immediately realised what he meant. We knew, from previous experience, that by moving the metal pointers on the globes we could travel across the planets. We did not understand how they worked but in certain circumstances, the time cavern could be controlled to not only move through time but also spatially as well.

We went to the Earth globe and found as expected the brass pointer over Midhurst.

"If this is working, we can just move the pointer and escape this inferno."

"But what about the bolts of lightning? We cannot stay here!" I said.

"I'll turn off Tesla's machine."

He went over to the console. But just as he reached for the lever I shouted, "No! James! It might remove the power from the globes and we will be stuck here! And we will be sucked into the Martian fight"

His hand hesitated. Then turning to me, with a look of despair, said, "Damn! You're right! It's Hobson's choice. Fried by Tesla's plasma or toasted by those Martian flame throwers."

One glance at the madness beyond the screens convinced me to trust our luck to the first option.

"So where shall we go?" I said.

"Anywhere but here."

And he moved the pointer.

J.

I didn't expect anything to happen when I pushed the pointer but to my relief, we immediately rose upwards as if we were in a lift with no walls.

We slowly left the battle below. As I looked down It was carnage. The floor was littered with broken smouldering tripods. Here and there survivors fought each other. Then the scene vanished as we went through the roof. Layers of white rock, sediment and sand passed us by then we shot out of the ground into the air leaving the ruined castle behind. However, the sense of relief was brief for across the Downs dozens of tripods were rising up out of the ground.

"We are too late they have already started their invasion!"

Blue and red beams of light shot from them accompanied by explosions. But I could see nothing fighting back. It took a few moments before I realised that they were attacking each other. I watched fascinated as the machines rose, exploded and fell.

"We must have started this. They must be on sort of automatic. When they started shooting each other to protect themselves from the plasma it must have triggered a defence mechanism."

"They are not very bright."

"Perhaps been buried in the ground for hundreds of years they were just programmed to attack and shoot anything that attacked them."

"Look! There are no more rising from the ground."

There was now no more than a few Tripods left chasing each other across the countryside.

"I reckon they'll all be finished in a few minutes."

A Plasma shot between Tesla and me with a resounding thwack as it hit a metal frame above the console.

Elizabeth shouted, "We have to turn it off James before we are electrocuted!"

"But we might fall back to Earth." I said.

"I will take my chances."

And before I could stop her, she ran over to the console and pulled the leaver.

There was one more crack of lightning which hit the console just missing her and then there was silence. Slowly the light which illuminated the cavern returned.

We stopped, hovering about a mile above the ground. I held my breath waiting to fall back to Earth but it did not. Instead, around us, outside the cavern, a gigantic circular structure began to materialise.

"What's this?" said James.

The structure became solid. It was a golden bronze disc, like a wheel with spokes, stretching from the rim to the walls of our cavern and was slowly rotating around us.

"My God! We are seeing the whole structure of the Time cavern! It must be over five hundred feet in diameter. Turning off the machine must have removed the field that hid it. We must be seeing the whole time machine."

I'd often wondered what was powering the cavern.

The only problem was, the Martians could see it as well for immediately three of the half dozen tripods left turned in our direction and started firing at us!

E.

Only a few moments before we had almost concluded that we had defeated the Martians. Now due to my stupidity we had revealed ourselves and had become the centre of their attention. Worse; the great machine which held us and powered or controlled the time cavern was being destroyed by the Martians for where their beams hit our vessel, pieces were breaking off and falling back to Earth.

There was only one thing to do. I had to undo my error. I ran to the console and pulled the lever again. I heard a reassuring hum and Mr Tesla's apparatus began to emit sparks again.

However, outside the Martians were coming closer and all six had joined in. More pieces of the great wheel broke away in the hail of fire. Then one of the spokes holding us cracked. We felt a judder then another. Green lights flashed on the console. Then I noticed the time clocks. They were oscillating back and forth through 1895.

I drew their attention to it.

James said, "The Martians must have caused some instability in time! God when are we going to end up?"

Mr Tesla said, "It seems to be hunting for some date or time. The fluctuations are getting smaller."

He was right. As we watched it the oscillations narrowed until it only showed March. Then it hovered around 13th March. Finally, the hours, minutes and seconds reduced to zero and stopped there.

Suddenly the walls or screens were jet black. It was almost impossible to focus on it. It reminded me of an art gallery James took me to see a simple painting of a black square. I am not a fan of modern art as he calls it and nor is he but, on this occasion, he wished to see a particular phenomenon. He told me the artist had used a special paint which absorbed all light. At first on regarding the painting it did indeed look like the artist had just painted a black square and at first I thought the public had been subjected to a confidence trick but no matter what light or illumination was shone upon it, nothing reflected! The eye couldn't focus on anything and you felt you were staring into nothingness. The walls were like that.

Suddenly Mr Tesla shouted. "We must get away!" and grabbing the Mars sphere moved the pointer but nothing happened. He turned to us.

"Were we actually travelling Mr Urquhart or was the vision

we saw like a motion picture?" he asked quite calmly as though observing an experiment.

James said, "We think we were moving. Though how I don't know. However, I'm not convinced the time cavern normally moves. I think it throws some form of projection."

"Are you saying that this place extrudes through space and time and we are carried with it?" said Tesla.

"I think it somehow manages to go outside time."

"Are we travelling just through space? Impossible!"

"That's what light does." James said.

"Forgive me but I think your reason is affected. Light travels at a certain speed. It is proven that light takes time to travel somewhere."

"Nope," said James, "The faster you travel, time slows down and at the speed of light, time reduces to zero."

"Time changes? Poppycock! Time is fixed."

"Is it? How long does it take you to get from London to New York?"

"About two weeks."

"And how do you measure that?"

"With a clock or count the number of days or nights."

"And how do you know how fast the clock moves or the days and nights?"

"It is self-evident."

"To an ordinary man, it is self-evident that the sun rises in the east and sets in the west. To the same man the sun goes around the Earth, but you know it is caused by the Earth spinning on its axis.

"But that is proved by observation

"And it is proved by observation that we and time and everything else travels at the speed of light."

Although this subject of space and time is always fascinating, I felt this was not the time for its discussion. In fact, I confess, I wished to strike them around their heads and bring them back to the reality before us.

I interjected. "May we return to the problem in hand. We are lost in a void with no vision of our surrounds and stuck in a particular time. What shall we do?"

They both looked at me then at each other. Mr Tesla was the first to speak.

"Who built this device?"

"I'm not sure," said James, regarding me with a smile indicating that he thanked me for pulling him out of a corner, "However, I do know that the Martians seem to be able to occupy five or more dimension. Somehow this cavern, ship or observatory, call it what you will, can travel outside or around our four-dimensional space-time. it is possible."

Do you mean the time cavern is no longer in Midhurst?" I said.

"Yes. We or the Martians have caused such a disturbance that the whole thing, whatever it is, has now left Earth.

"Then how do we get home?"

J.

The three of us were now starring at a black wall with Tesla's machine standing silent and two globes which had lost their glow. The time clocks registered midnight on 13th March 1895. My first conclusion was our time machine was broken, and we were stranded outside time and space for ever. Even worse, I was feeling hungry.

None of these facts helped me think what to do next and this is why you should always have an enquiring, intelligent Victorian wife with you when confronted with a situation like this.

She was a holding piece of what looked like a triangular

piece of brass. It was about a foot long.

"What's that from?"

"It is the piece of debris that came through the wall when the Martian's attacked. I thought if this could come through then perhaps there is a hole through which we might pass."

She handed it to me. "Do you know from what it is made?"

It looked like brass but was very light and felt like a plastic. It was also warm to the touch. The surface was very smooth but when I looked closely I couldn't see my reflection. It was reflecting light but not in the normal way.

I passed it to Tesla who turned it over in hands a number of times then bit it.

"Interesting there is no mark. It feels soft but hard at the same time. It is not of any material I have come across." "And handed it back to me.

"Well I don't know what it's made of either," I said, "but I think I'll keep hold of it. Perhaps Wells can help."

"Do you think w should find the hole this object made?"

"It may not have made a hole. It might have just passed through like a stone through liquid." I said.

"Then there is only one way to find out." said Elizabeth and she walked to the wall in the generally direction from which the object had come from.

We followed.

After about five minutes of carefully prodding the wall with no effect again, I suddenly thought that the piece of shrapnel might help.

I said, "I'm going to see if I push this triangle through the wall. Perhaps it has special properties that allow it to pass through."

I pressed it against the wall, and it slid through like a hot knife through butter.

"I'm going to try and make a small hole with it try and push something through."

I cut about a foot square and took off my hat and pressed it against the place where I'd made the incision. To my surprise not to say fright, the hat and my hand went through the wall. I immediately pulled my hand out, letting go of the hat.

My hand felt alright and I hadn't felt a thing.

"So, it seems, Mr Urquhart," said Tesla. "If we make a hole big enough we can escape."

"But where to? And is there a breathable atmosphere?"

Elisabeth grabbed my hand and examined it. "There are no lesions James. Maybe we will be safe."

"I suppose I could poke my head in."

There expressions indicated that this would be an excellent idea. So, I enlarged the hole, which I couldn't see, held my breath, closed my eyes and pushed my face into where I thought I'd cut the hole.

Nothing. I pulled out my head.

"What's there?" said Tesla.

"Couldn't see a thing. There must be something here. The plasma got out and that piece of shrapnel got in here. I'm going to cut it larger."

"I hope the air does not escape," said Elizabeth.

A bead of sweat formed on my head, not least because if the air was going to escape, I had no idea how to plug the hole again. However, the absence of any draft or wind suggested that whatever was on the other side was at the same pressure as the cavern.

I enlarged the hole with the golden shard until it was big enough to step through.

"OK." I said, "we are all going to hold hands. I'll go first, then Elizabeth then You Tesla. Any problems pull like hell!"

We each grasped a hand then we walked towards the blank wall.

209

I didn't feel a thing. It was as though there was nothing there.

E.

We stood or floated in total blackness grasping each other's hand firmly. At first I could see nothing but as I became accustomed to the darkness I could see faintly a large object around which was some kind of supporting frame.

Mr Tesla nearly made me jump out my skin.

"It is my laboratory! There is my resonance coil!"

He let go of my hand and rushed into the darkness and disappeared.

I realised I wasn't holding anyone's hand.

"James! Where are you?"

"Here!" he shouted, gratifyingly close. "Stay still. And keep talking I will come to you."

I felt his hand then his arms were around me squeezing me tight, which was a little embarrassing because as I planted a kiss on his neck the lights came on.

Thankfully Mr Tesla ignored our position.

"We have arrived before I switched on the apparatus."

Before we could stop him, he ran over to the power supply.

"What are you doing?" shouted James.

Mr Tesla ignored him and grabbing two thick cable proceeded to yank them out of the console

"I am making sure it the oscillator is completely detached from it's power supply just in case it starts again."

Soddenly I heard a bell chime, then another. We all turned to the other wall where there was a large mechanical clock. Its hands were on midnight.

We watched it in silence as it struck midnight then noticed the minute hand move forward a minute.

"Time has started again!"

"Then we may be back in our own time again."

"And perhaps we have stopped the shift in time."

\-------------------

J.

Tesla was good enough to put us up at his pad. He had only one bed, which obviously, we gave to Elizabeth and I dozed on a sofa while Tesla fell fast asleep in an armchair.

In the morning, I awoke to find he'd disappeared. I was about to wake Elizabeth to tell her we were now abandoned somewhere in New York without a single dollar when Tesla returned clutching a newspaper.

His face was in shock.

"What's the matter?"

"My Laboratory! It is destroyed! All my work, up in flames!"

I sat him down in the arm chair and grabbed the paper. It was the New York Herald for Thursday March 14th 1895. I scanned the front page. Nothing. Just adverts. I turned to the next page. Nothing about a fire there either. I began to suspect Tesla had had some kind of brain fever.

Then Elizabeth, who had now been fully woken by the commotion came up to me and said, "What is the matter? Is Mr Tesla ill?"

"I think so. He brought this paper which he says claims his lab has been destroyed by fire but I can't find anything on it."

She took the paper from me. Looked at what I was reading and said, "Oh James! Don't you now that in my time the real news was often a few pages in?

" There on this page. It says... oh, gosh! It is true! Look!"

And there on page 5 at the top;

\----------------

FRUITS OF GENIUS
WERE SWEPT AWAY.
By a Fire the Noted Electrician,
Nikola Tesla, Loses Mechan-
-isms of Inestimable Value.

I didn't know whether to be relieved that the fire had happened or feel sorry for Tesla.

E.

Mr Tesla was very ill. All his life's work had been destroyed. We stayed with him for a few days, nursing him back to health, embarrassingly at his expense, for we did not have any American monies, and fending off the reporters and journalists who came to his door.

After five days, he was walking again and during the late evenings when the streets were empty, we convinced him to take to the airs.

Soon his enthusiasm for his work returned and he commenced writing and sending letters to all and sundry. After about two weeks James and I had become full time secretaries and dispatchers of mail and our presence on the streets was beginning to attract attention. Seeing that he seemed to be on his own feet again I broached the subject of our retuning home.

He was most generous in his reward for our help.

Chapter Twenty-two

J.

There are many old photos of dockyards on the internet. What they don't show you is the smell, and noise of thousands of people, baggage handlers, carriages, horses.

Elizabeth and I were in sitting in a carriage with wall-to-wall buttoned upholstery. We had joined a line of similar carriages at the Customs post for Tesla had bought us Cabin tickets on the RMS Campania for Liverpool and we were, thankfully, in the posh people's queue. Apparently, it only cost $450 with a servant thrown in. The downside was that we had to arrive at the quay by six o'clock in the morning and Mr Tesla's farewell party, which finished about three in the morning had left both of us with a bit of a headache.

Tesla had provided us with a carriage which Elizabeth said was just sufficient for our needs, or her needs. For, she reminded me that our voyage might last seven or eight days and during that time a lady could not be seen in the same dress twice. Given that this rule applied both day and evening wear, I wondered whether we should have hired an extra carriage. As for me, it seems that in 1895 as long as I turned up in a good pair of underpants and wearing a dicky-bow I would be accepted in polite circles.

I was just about to renounce my socialist principles and join the 'good life' when to the right of us further down the quay the doors of a large shed opened and a large sea of people immerged. As they flowed passed us, I noticed that they were separated from us by a fence. I had never seen such poverty first hand. Most of them were carrying their own baggage. They reminded me of those long lines of refugees or displaced persons I'd seen in those old black and white news reels from the second world war except now in colour I saw its reality.

These had left their country in the hope of a new and better life. Many of them looked in wonder at our row of carriages from which many ladies and gents were already alighting dressed in all their morning finery and assisted by servants retrieving and carrying their luggage.

When our turn came to get out, I'm sorry to say, that I did my upmost to pretend I didn't notice the crowds trudging by.

The Campania was sitting in a long birth. It didn't look very big. And certainly not big enough to cross the Atlantic. There were two tall funnels painted red and black which I remembered were the colours of the Cunard Line. Beside it scores of carriages, hundreds of grey clad men handling luggage and provisions into the cargo bays. Behind them, waiting, dozens of open horse-drawn trucks laden with coal to fire the boilers.

We eventually managed to get through the customs posts with our tickets. Thankfully no one asked for passports.

When we had climbed the gang plank to our surprise we were met by our own personal valet, who introduced himself as Peters who told us he would be looking after us on the voyage. I suspected that his agency gave out appropriate names which would be acceptable to society.

He led us down a panelled corridor and opened the door into what I can only describe as the most opulent Victorian entrance hall I'd ever seen. Everything, and I mean everything was covered in ornate art nouveau woodwork and in the centre a large and wide staircase which I thought would normally be reserved for royalty but apparently was just reserved for us. At the top, we came to another floor with lounges. Elizabeth said that although she had never been in a London Club, but from what her cousin had described this place was definitely at the exclusive end of the market.

Eventually, after walking for about a mile along a corridor lined with paintings of famous ship's captains and sea battles on thick Axminster carpets we came to our room. I say room for first we had to walk through a salon complete with sofas comfy chairs, port holes and a fireplace! Apparently, we could light a fire if we were a bit cold!

As for the bedroom, well, it was wall to wall wood panelling, two sofas, a massive four poster bed in which I think two people could easily lose touch with each other and a drinks cabinet already lined with a sufficient range of liquors which would keep you permanently sozzled for at least three return journey. I said to Elizabeth, "If we get back home I want you to redesign our bedroom just like this."

To which she replied, "And when I've finished where shall we put the other rooms?"

Then I remembered our luggage. I was just about to apologise to Peters that I'd left our luggage on the carriage and I'd have to go back for it when a small bell rang. Peters immediately returned to our living room, opened the door and after gently reminding me that that onerous task was not my job, two livered men and a maid servant came in with our luggage. Before I could pick any of it up, I was ushered into a small room which I discovered was my own clothes cupboard while the maid servant took Elizabeth to hers. This team then proceeded to get out all our clothes and hang or fold them expertly in the appropriate spaces within, I am sure in less than a minute.

When they'd finished, I gave them a ten dollar note each, mainly as a reward for their show of expertise. Their eyes popped when they saw the notes and tried to ask for less but I wasn't having it. I needed to cleans my conscience a bit, though I didn't tell them that.

Peters, seeing that everything was in place, ask permission

to leave after drawing attention to a bell push which apparently would have him at our side within seconds. From what I'd seen so far, I believed him. I imagined he had small chamber attached to our rooms from which he could leap out at a moment's notice. I tried to give him a tip but he refused saying that Mr Tesla had more than adequately rewarded him on the condition that he saw to our every whim.

From what I'd seen in the last half hour I decided I wouldn't need any more whims for the rest of our lives.

E.

There is nothing like a hot steaming bath in which one's body fits comfortably, followed by soft warm towels. Although, I confess, my family is of reasonable means, I must admit as James often puts it, I was a little out of my class.

Mr Tesla's generosity had not only bought us a first-class cabin but allowed me to replace my complete wardrobe. James on seeing my selection and quantity wondered how New Yorkers would find clothes to buy after I'd finished. However, when on the quay, he saw the luggage of the other first-class carriages he decided that I was quite frugal in my spending and promised never to complain about my travelling requirements again. He is usually quite difficult when purchasing clothes, preferring instead his gardening garments but I could not miss out on this opportunity to provide him with a proper attire. For I wished him not to keep borrowing from my father's wardrobe which required clips and stich to fit.

I eventually persuaded him to visit one of fashionable emporiums and buy seven sets of suits, shirts, socks and shoes. I was pleased to see once dressed properly that he quite enjoyed it and he did look quite fetching, though understandably he refused the underwear. He has reason for

I would recommend to any lady of my time who finds herself in the twenty-first century to immediately 'snap-up' all the undergarments she can afford before she returns home. This especially applies to 'bras' which keep one's breasts in wonderful condition. Also, if I may be so bold, if chosen with caution can aid in drawing attention to one you desire. Though the wrong colour can attract undue to attention. As an aside, from a particular experience, for which I am indebted to James' sister, Jill, they must always be worn underneath a dress or blouse unless you are participating in a pre-nuptial party where it seems it is derigueur even in public to wear on the outside of one's clothes. I have also discovered that they can be a source of much hilarity amongst our men-folk and on occasion when they have banded together for an exceedingly late evening at a hostelry borrow their wives' bras and wear them on display for all to see. I am only aware of this because one evening Jill and I saw James, Sean and their friends walking past our home one night wearing such items. I have still not obtained a satisfactory explanation from James on this nor where the bras were obtained!

But to return.

About eight o'clock a bell rang summoning dinner.

I was not quite ready for I was unsure which evening dress was suitable.

James, who was now in evening dress said, "Well, you can't complain you've nothing to wear."

"I am a little nervous for I am a little out of this society."

"You are! What about me? Tell you what I'll get Peters to give us some advice."

"I prefer the maid."

"Peters' paid to look after us. I'll trust him."

And before I could protest he pressed the bell and Peters instantly appeared.

I must confess this valet was perfect. Where Mr Tesla found him I do not know. James hoped he was the original inspiration for a gentleman's gentleman in a series of book by a Mr Wodehouse he had read and said he looked forward to his remedy or cure if we had an exceedingly late evening. It was only later that I understood what he meant. With James permission, Peters, with impeccable deference to my sex, gave me advice on my attire and after a few adjustments of clothing pronounced that I was ready for the evening.

He then with an apology said, "You will find, if it is your first trip that you will meet those with money, those with class, those with both and those with neither. I would suggest that you be yourselves. In that way, you will find people to your liking."

He then looked a little embarrassed as though he was speaking out of turn and in reply for his good advice thanked him for sharing his experience. This time James managed to put a ten dollar note in his breast pocket.

J.

We eventually left our room about eight thirty. Elizabeth looked ravishing in layers of yellow embroidered silk and showing a nice square cleavage. However, she declined my offer to stay in our rooms and have dinner brought to us.

We were only half way down the corridor wondering which way to go when Peters appeared out of a door and offered to take us to the restaurant. For some reason, I felt a little unsteady on my feet. Peters noticed and gently held my arm.

"It's OK Sir. The ship is leaving port. Once we are out in the waters the movement will become more manageable."

I hoped he was right. I usually took sea sickness pills just to cross the channel.

Eventually after passing a number of richly furnished and panelled lounges already occupied by a variety of smoking gentlemen, we arrived at the dining room, or banqueting hall as I would prefer to call it for it was occupied by over a hundred tables, all white clothed and silvered. Judging by the raucous noise several parties had already started and long tailed waiters were scurrying about with trays of food and drink trying to satisfy the guests needs. I was just wondering where to sit when Peters beckoned us to the other end of the hall. It seemed a very long hall and I was conscious of many faces turning to us no doubt wondering who we were and how we'd been let on the ship. Eventually we were guided to a table where, judging by his naval uniform, sat the Captain of the ship!

E.

Although I have travelled to the continent on package boats, I had never been on a transatlantic steamship before and to be taken to the Captain's table filled me with trepidation not least because he was sitting on a table by himself. However, Peters introduced us to the Captain by saying that we were the couple who had nursed Mr Tesla back to health.

"Ah! Mr and Mrs Urquhart. Please sit down. Are your rooms adequate and comfortable?"

James replied that he was very satisfied and said to my embarrassment that he never stayed in a bedroom bigger than his house before.

Luckily the Captain was very kind to us and made much of our helping Mr Tesla. It seems that as a man who had spent his life trying to navigate high seas by stars or luck, he was very encouraging of the likes of Mr Tesla who could provide a wireless communication across the world. The mention of the scientific methods of Mr Tesla allowed James to come into his element where withe aid of the wine which accompanied our meal and the port after he was able to give the Captain a detailed description of Mr Tesla's experiments. The Captain was much fascinated by James 'view' of the future where ships could navigate by signals from the shore. Though when he mentioned that one day ships would navigate by communication by satellites in space, he suggested politely that perhaps James should take up fictional writings of the form of Jules Verne where his imagination could be given the freedom it desired.

About one o'clock a small orchestra started up and I was very flattered to be offered the first dance by the Captain. Although a little nervous, the looks of admiration if not envy from the surrounding tables relaxed me considerably and I must confess my confidence was much improved. Luckily by the time James asked to dance, the floor was filled with people and his performance, despite my previous instructions on the waltz and gavotte, for the most part, went unnoticed.

J.

We left the dining room after a couple of dances to a Palm Court Orchestra to preserve Elizabeth's toes. It was the third time she had tried to teach me a waltz and being a little worse for wear, no doubt because of the motion of the ship and not the port as she suggested, I decided we should retire.

We eventually found our rooms with aid of Peters who despite our protestations that we knew where we were going, appeared at every wrong turning to guide us along the correct path.

Passing through the first room we both flopped on the bed. Elizabeth looked a little unwell.

"Are you OK?"

"I fear I drunk a little too much wine."

"Well let's get this gear off and get into this enormous bed. I'm stuffed"

"You should try wearing stays."

"I thought you didn't wear them."

"Normally I do not, but I was a little nervous of my reception and decided to comply with fashion. My stomach is not speaking to me."

"With your waist-line! Most girls in my time would dream of having your shape.

Let's get it off then."

I'd discovered that most Victorian women did not lace themselves up until they achieved a waist line of 18 inches. Like the monocle, it was a fashion. Apparently, it was normally just to tightened enough to be comfortable. Unfortunately, Elizabeth had tried to go for the thinnest waist on the ship.

I'm not quite sure how the maid had got it on but if anyone had come into the bedroom while Elizabeth was bent over the bed with me kneeling on top trying to unpluck the laces, the conversation would have been interesting.

Eventually it was removed accompanied by a sigh of relief from both of us. She didn't object when I threw it out the port hole.

Afterwards we both agreed that was enough exertion for one night and without getting into pyjamas we climbed into bed and were fast asleep in seconds.

E.

We awoke about mid-day and ordered a light lunch, brought by a maid who seemed not to mind we received her in bed. After we both fell asleep again.

It was about six o'clock that we eventually rose. Feeling that it would be rude to miss dinner we prepared ourselves again.

When we entered the dining hall a waiter immediately met us and guided us to a table near the stage. I noticed that the Captain was at his table but receiving other guests. I imagine that on these voyages he had a lot of people to entertain.

J.

After dinner, we retired to one of the salons but the cigar smoke and motion of the boat plus possibly the wine made me feel a bit queasy. I suggested that we take some air and we staggered up the stairs, through the main lounge and on to the promenade deck. A few couples in evening dress were strolling along the deck. Somewhere a gramophone started playing a waltz and a couple started a smoochy slow dance.

The air was clear and the stars twinkled brightly. I'd never seen so many. I searched for a planet but none were to be found. To the rear, I could see the white wake of the ship stretching out into the distance.

"Do you think we will get back to your time?"

She was wearing a green silk dress embroidered with peacocks and other birds which possibly the artist had never seen but I did not mind because whoever had cut it knew exactly how to emphasise her shape.

"I don't know and in truth I don't really mind at the moment. I'm enjoying the pleasure of this luxury."

"Me to. We could not have planned a better holiday and we will have almost a week to ourselves with no distractions."

I felt a weight fall from my shoulders.

"Your right. Let's walk down to the front deck and watch the stars."

As we sauntered along with the sound of the waltz floating

in the air I was sure I saw Peters once or twice pretending to be busy.

"When do you think we will get back home?" she said.

"My calculation is about 3rd^h of April."

"That will be about three days after we left my home."

"We better make sure we don't arrive before."

"Why? Do you think we will meet ourselves?"

"I don't know whether we can. I'm more worried about the confusion it will cause."

"Yes. I agree. If we do find ourselves in that situation, then perhaps we should extend our holiday. We still have monies from Mr Tesla spare."

"You better save that just in case I need to replenish your clothes again."

"I do have enough for at least seven more of your adventures which even you may have difficulty devising ways to ruin them."

"It may surprise you but I'd like to avoid any more adventures."

She slid her arm into mine. I felt the warm silk against me and pulled her closer.

We eventually reached the forward deck and leaned over the rail. Two great searchlights shone forward. I wondered how far north we were. I couldn't see any icebergs.

I looked up at the stars in the jet-black sky. The Milky Way arched overhead so clear. I slowly followed it down. It stopped some twenty degrees above the horizon.

"That's interesting. There must be a fog bank ahead for I can't see any stars there. Look," I said pointing to the horizon.

"Yes. It must be fog or mist but I can't see it."

"There's no moon to shine on it. I presume they haven't got radar. I don't want to find us in fog in the middle of field of icebergs,"

223

"Oh, I'd love to see one."

I was just wondering whether to mention the Titanic when the search lights picked up the fog. A great blast came from the ships fog horn which nearly made us both jump in the air.

For about ten minutes we watched the fog come closer and closer. Wisps began to pass by the ship. The stars disappeared. The gramophone had stopped playing.

I said, "I think we better go back inside. I believe these north Atlantic fogs can be quite cold."

We turned away from the rail and proceeded to walk slowly back down the deck. Other people must have had the same idea because the deck was now deserted. The fog was quite close now. It was very quiet. Too quiet.

Elizabeth noticed as well, "Can you here the engines?"

I listened. I could hear nothing. "Maybe the engines have stopped for some reason. Hope they haven't spotted an iceberg"

Another vision of the Titanic came to me. For some reason, I wondered if I could get into one of Elizabeth's dresses. The fog was now rolling on to the deck. We both decided to walk a little faster and closer to the cabin walls.

"I'm not quite sure where we came out." I whispered, "I think before this stuff gets any thicker we'll go through the first door we find."

"I agree. It is unusual for I do not feel cold or damp."

I tried a couple of doors. They were locked. The silence was beginning to worry me.

I felt her hand reach and grasp mine, "I feel we are lost James."

I agreed but didn't say anything. Then suddenly a door opened and there to our relief was Peters in his full evening dress wearing his relaxing smile.

"Excuse my interruption Sir, but I thought you were in need

of assistance."

His calmness was reassuring.

"Too right Peters. We've managed to lose our way."

"I do not want to contradict you Sir, but I don't believe you have Sir. I think you will find you have arrived at where you wish to be."

And he stood aside and beckoned us in.

As I went through the cabin door I was quite surprised by the room's familiarity. It took a moment to realise that the presence of my sister, Wells and Elizabeth's father told me that we were no longer on the ship.

Chapter Twenty-three

E.

The first words from James' sister did not reduce the shock of finding myself in the parlour of my home in Hamgreen.

"What you doing back? I thought you were going to Midhurst. And why are you wearing a monkey suit Jim? And, wow! Where did you get that dress Elizabeth? I want one."

Seeing no reply from us except the stunned expressions on our faces she said, "Are you alright? You look like you've seen another ghost."

Still not receiving a response, my father asked where was Mr Tesla.

I noticed James was shaking his head in disbelief. I decided to take hold, though it was not easy.

"We have been to Midhurst, destroyed the Martian tripods, then transported to Mr Tesla's laboratory in New York, nursed him back to health after his laboratory burnt down then took a steamship back to England at his generous expense during which journey we went through a door into our cabin and found ourselves back to here."

"Any questions?" said James.

Ii was our turn to be met by a stunned silence.

"How long have we been away?" I asked.

"Ten minutes," said Jill. "Would you like some tea?"

"No thanks." said James. "We've had dinner, danced for an hour and it's two o'clock in the morning. I also feel a hangover coming on and I want to go to bed."

Instead of agreeing to what I thought was a reasonable request we were subjected to a barrage of questions whose replies, I'm sure took over an hour.

Eventually they agreed that we might be a little fatigued and we could go to bed after James fell asleep on the chair.

I woke him gently. He looked around dazed and said, "Are we still on the ship? I had a weird dream that we were your home with...."

He saw the others sitting around him.

"Oh God. It's real. I was really looking forward to that four-poster bed again."

He rose off the chair and grimaced. "Ooh me head! What did I drink?"

"The port again James."

"Oh dear. Can I go to bed now?"

"Yes you can." And with not a little help from Jill we got him upstairs.

J.

We slept for over twelve hours and as consequence we arrived down stairs just in time for lunch. I asked Lilly if I could have a full English breakfast to which she replied, "It is already cooking on the stove Mr Urquhart and will be here in a few minutes."

I said, "Lilly you're a star. Do you want to come and back and cook for us?"

"I think Lizzy can do a far more adequate job than me."

Elizabeth gave me a look which indicated I should agree with her.

Then just as I was about to get my first sausage in my mouth, everyone else turned up and just in case we thought we'd dreamt our escapade we were subjected to the same bunch of questions again. When they'd finished and I was still trying to eat my second sausage I decided to ask some questions of my own, starting with Wells.

"Did you plan all this?"

"No. All I knew was the Martians needed you."

"What world are we in now?"

"The world you expected. The disjoint in time has been removed."

"How do you know?"

Elizabeth's father helped out, "When the post arrived this morning I asked if he could describe Midhurst for me. I am afraid by his expression he thought me dodderier then I looked but humoured me. However, he did wonder for my health when I asked if there were any electric trams."

"And what about your wife, Wells?"

"She is in the kitchen."

"So, she has stayed."

I wondered what happened to the other Wells but decided best not to ask. For all I knew after the last couple of weeks I was talking to the other one.

Then Jill said, "What about the Martian invasion? Do you think it might still happen?"

I looked at Wells who said as though it was of no consequence. "I have heard nothing,"

It seems we were back in our world again or least Elizabeth's.

Then I remembered Peters.

"We had this chap, Peters he called himself, who claimed he'd been hired by Tesla to look after us on the ship. He was the one who opened the door on the ship that led us here. Do you know him?"

Wells said, "Do you remember the Magic Shop you visited in London about a year you began to time travel."

"You mean that old shop full of amazing steampunk like curious devices."

"Yes," then he turned to Elizabeth's father, "And do you remember, Mr Bicester, your father's visit to that shop on the

Pulteney Bridge in Bath?"

He nodded. Elizabeth's grandfather, being a little worse for wear and broke had gone in to a shop on the bridge and by the time he left found himself the owner of the lodge at Hamgreen and also all the time problems that went with it.

Wells continued, "Peters is the proprietor of the Magic Shop or as he likes to call it 'The Genuine Magic Shop'. It is a wondrous place though it has no place."

"What do you mean, it has no place?" said Elizabeth.

"It materialises when someone is thought to have the abilities to alter time."

"And where is this Magic Shop now?" she said.

"Where or when ever he detects someone who might be interested in his trade. Once he has someone the shop vanishes"

"That's why I never found that shop again," I said, "Who is he then?"

"He is like us but can travel outside time and space. It allows him to move from place or time to another."

"Like the Martians?"

"I believe he is a descendant of the original Martians who came to Earth."

"You mean we've interbred with the Martian's?" said Jill.

"It is possible."

"That must have been an interesting coupling." She replied, "Mind you, Jim, it could explain some of the blokes I've known. Come out of nowhere and disappear without trace."

"Do you think there are more like him in the world?" said Elizabeth.

I suddenly imagined thousands of them all over the world living incognito waiting for God knows what. Then I thought I'd been watching to many Scifi TV shows.

"I do not know," said Wells, "He has never mentioned

children. Perhaps he is a one off so to speak, an experiment. Perhaps there are many."

I was just managing to eat the last piece of black pudding having wiped it in the egg yoke when I suddenly thought of my car. I grabbed Elisabeth and pulling her from her seat, spilling her tea in the process on her dress, rushed to the front door. I opened it and there it was. Relief!

When Elizabeth saw it she grabbed me. "Oh James! We can go home. But I must...."

"Say goodbye to your father?"

"Yes. Thank you." And off she went.

I shouted out, "And don't forget my sister!"

I looked at my car. Just five paces and we would be on our way home.

E.

I was literally pushed by James and Jill into the car. Before I had attached the safety-straps James had ignited the engine and raced the car up the drive shedding stones in all directions. He did not slow down until we arrived at the highway at Cocking and joined some a convoy of cars who despite his language refused to increase their speed to accommodate him.

It was a relief to find ourselves in our own time however I noticed, even though we were on a familiar road, James was continually regarding the rear-view mirror in expectation, as he later told me, of seeing a horde of Martian tripods following us.

It was only when we had passed through Lavant and reached the outskirts of Chichester, and I began to think of our home and comfort when I realised with some shock that on going through that cabin door I had foregone almost fourteen of the most expensive and beautiful dresses I could never afford to wear. I could only presume when the chamber maid discovered them she would be able to retire on the proceeds of their sale. Such is the trials of time travel.

When we eventually arrived home after suffering two traffic jams, a road works controlled by two men who did not know their red sign from their green, we rushed down the path to the front door only to find that James had left his keys on the ship. Luckily, before he volunteered to shin up a rather rusty drain pipe and try and attempt to squeeze through the bedroom fanlight. Jill remembered she thought she might have a spare key. It was eventually found by emptying the contents of her handbag on the ground. On looking at the large collection of objects, tissues, sweet wrappers etc., I made a mental note to clear out mine at the earliest opportunity before James found an excuse to rummage in it. For I am sure he would use it as a defence on my comments on the contents of garage and shed.

The key fitted, the door opened and we piled in. Letters spilled on to the floor but we ignored them and went straight into the living room, where, neatly parcelled on the coffee table like a Boxing Day treat, were a pile of large brown paper parcels. We looked at each other and then James went over and opened one. A yellow evening gown spilled out. I recognised it immediately.

"It is the clothes from our voyage James! How did they get here?"

"Don't ask me. But it looks like we are going to have to buy another cupboard."

We then proceeded to open all the parcels like children at a Christmas party.

Jill held up a red silk dress and pressed to her body. "Oh, these are so beautiful. If we find ourselves back in your time again you must let me borrow one."

I agreed. Then James who was examining his newly acquired wardrobe noticed a small card on the table.

"What's this? Oh, it looks like one of your Victorian calling cards."

He handed it to me. On the front was a neat coloured drawing of the Campania. I turned it over. There was what seemed to be a small advertisement in flowery print. I held it closer and nearly fainted. It read.

'The Genuine Magic Shop,
South Street,
Chichester.'

And underneath in a green copperplate pen.

'Please visit.
If you have the time.
Peters'

They both noticed my concern and came over to me.

"Are you OK? What does it say?"

When James read it, his visage was as mine.

"I'm going get some matches and carefully burn it." he said, "and pretend we know never saw it."

I was just about to agree when Jill stopped us.

"Don't! It's come from a magic shop! Maybe destroying it will invoke some trick on us or make us disappear in a puff of smoke!"

For a moment, James held it in his hand, turning it over and over slowly.

"You could be right."

Then he walked over to the sideboard and placed it out of

sight in a draw.

"I think we'll just leave it alone in there and go and have a cup of tea."

Later we returned to the living room and carefully repacked the clothes and took them up to the attic and placed and sealed them in a tea chest for we were convinced that they might be enchanted as well.

Epilogue

E.

We have returned to our quiet and peaceful life again. For over a month we have not been visited upon by time travellers or Mr Wells nor transported to who knows where or when.

But then, we do not open that sideboard draw nor enquire of the box of those beautiful garments in the attic.

The End

Other Books by Bruce Macfarlane

from the
Time Travel Diaries of James Urquhart and Elizabeth
Bicester

Book 1 Out of Time

The first diaries of the humorous and sometimes romantic time travel adventures of James Urquhart, minor science lecturer living in 2015 and Elizabeth Bicester, lady of leisure, whom he stumbles upon at a cricket match at Hamgreen in 1873. Despite their banter regarding each other's manners they manage through incredible feats of illogical deduction and with not a little help from James Maxwell, H. G. Wells, the Martians and some strange time devices, to save the world.

Book 2 A Drift Out of Time

In this volume, they have returned home to find they are not only in an alternative future but a different aspect of themselves. To get back to their world they must travel between Mars and Earth, drifting across time and space, until eventually they reach home and discover who the Martians really are.

Book 3 A House Out of Time

Once again, the intrepid couple have "retired' to a quiet life of ease in an alternative world after helping the Martians save the Earth and their own planet. Unfortunately, Elizabeth thought it would be a good idea to visit her ancestral home at Hamgreen to see what had become of it.

….Such is the curiosity of women.

Book 4 The Space Between Time

In these extracts from the Time Travel Diaries we find the intrepid couple enjoying a peaceful and romantic picnic by the River Rother when a motor launch turns up complete with Mr Wells.

Apparently, a certain Mr Tesla has conducted one of his electro-magnetic experiments which has fractured time and dumped everyone in an alternative world of 1895. The problem is that only a few people have noticed the difference.

Mr Wells wondered if James and Elizabeth would like to help.

Short Stories

Three Tales Out of Time

If you ever find yourself going out with a Victorian lady and you feel the need to impress her with your romantic skills, I would suggest taking her night clubbing in Hartlepool, camping in Cornwall or touring in the remote parts of France should be immediately crossed off your list.

Short and almost "true" stories from the Time Travel Diaries of James Urquhart and Elizabeth Bicester

Notes on Arthurian Literature.

This book contains my notes on Arthurian literature examine the origins of Arthur and the historical events associated with him.

It also reviews the Celtic origins of the Grail stories and the significance of their appearance at the time of the crusades after the fall of Jerusalem in 1009 and recapture by Godfrei de Boullion in 1099 and their re-emergence in Mallory's Mort D'Arthur after the fall of Constantinople in 1454.

Subjects covered in the book are;

The Origins of Arthur.

Possible Links to Historical Events.

Problems with Dating Events in the 5th and 6th Centuries.

Climatic and Astronomical Phenomenon in 5th and 6th Century Britain.

The Appearance of the Grail Stories.

Historical Characters and Events in the Grail Stories.

Celtic and Other Origins of the Grail and the Grail Characters.

Malory and the Tales of King Arthur.

.

About the Author

Bruce is a retired Health Physicist who lives with his wife on the south coast of England, just a few minutes' walk from the sea. When he's not researching King Arthur, he's out walking on the South Downs with his wife and his friends trying to remember all the names of the flowers and mushrooms his wife has identified.

When it's raining he can be found sometimes in his "shed" as his wife calls it, trying to master new jazz chords.

A life of writing scientific reports and reading early science fiction, especially the genre of time travel such as the works of Anderson, Simak and Wells encouraged him to start writing his own novels about the adventures of a modern man and a Victorian lady whom he met at a cricket match in 1873.

His stories have been described as "Tom Holt meets P.G. Wodehouse meets Philip K. Dick meets Fortean Times."

You can get more information on this and his other books and hobbies at: his blog at:

https://timetdiaries.wordpress.com

Or you can visit our website at:

http://www.aldwickpublishing.com/